STAYING ALIVE

A horror Novel

By

John Edwards

ISBN 9781638230496

Table of Contents

Chapter 1

Sometimes life doesn't always work out the way you want it to. Sometimes it does. But, it all depends on the person. Well at least that's what I think.

But not everyone thinks the same thing. Some may think that one little negative thing that happens in their lives just destroys everything, they become dark and distance from the world and everyone they know and love. And forget about the thought of living. In some cases, there are those who can learn to cope with it. And be able to live on with the negative memory. Though this is my opinion, I cannot empathize to those people. But I do understand them a little. But, there are those who live life happily. No matter what happens they always pull through. Almost acting like nothing has happened. Like it never happened to begin with.

I am kind of in between those two types of people. I don't exactly think about life that deeply. I do care about mine and those around me. But there are times when the days get heavier and heavier, and you have no idea how to live with it. Some think I'm strange for feeling this way but...that's how I am.

You know that feeling when, one day things don't feel the same. Like the world just changed a little and you felt it. Almost like you're the only one to notice it. I don't get it myself but, today of all days the feeling was stronger than usual. School wasn't always my favourite place to be in. sitting for almost a half an hour listening to the teacher rant on about the subject you're currently in. Most of the time I don't even pay attention, I usually spend the class time staring out the window and almost most of

1

the time the teacher doesn't notice me. I'd hate to embarrass myself in the middle of a lecture. Particularly math. It isn't my strongest subject, but I know enough of it to pass me on to the next grade. All I could hear was the soft ticking of the clock that hung right above the door inside the classroom. It was rather small for such a large classroom. You could barely notice it up there besides its ticking. I peered out of the glass window into the barely lit hallway. There was no one walking about, except for those people that monitor them.

I turned my head to the side and directed my gaze towards Elise. My best friend you could say. She's not at all like me. She's the type of person that would actually pay attention in class. No matter how many times I'd try to distract her, it would only piss her off. Which would result to either being ignored or slapped. In any case I'd much rather not liked to be slapped.

As class went on like normal, my hands began to shake. The feeling had grown stronger. My head began to throb, I had chills running down my spine. That one feeling you get when something bad is about to happen. Though I wish it would never result into something like that.

But, once that intercom came on, my instincts kicked in. The throbbing in my head had faded, the chills vanished, and the constant trembling of my hands subsided. I was ready for whatever was about to happen.

The room silenced, but in that stillness the impudent ticking of the clock filled the room. I was ready, but was everyone else?

The intercom began to make static noises. It pierced our ears. The pain wasn't so bad but for others it might be. It only lasted for a couple of seconds until it stopped. My body was tense. What is it that I should be doing now? Should I ask her to bring "that" out now or later? I was waiting for the right time to say it.

"Jade..." Elise turned to me concerned. I gave her a small grin and nodded to her that I was fine. She sighed and looked back at the intercom speaker. Inside the silence I could hear the soft hums of someone, or something speaking into the intercom. Class time had stopped. Even the teacher ended his lecture. I sat still, waiting for the right time. I may be wrong but, I could feel it. There just might be something wrong with the intercom or someone hit the ON button by accident and has no idea that it's on. Right?

"I'm right...right"? I could spend all day thinking of different possibilities on this matter if I had the time. But right now, it could be either one of my theories. The intercom began to make more noises. It wasn't the static noise from earlier, but the distinct growl that sounded like a tortured animal. It shrieked in pain. It didn't sound like something a normal human being could possibly make. I gritted my teeth. I tightened my fist, the nails on my fingers almost piercing my skin. I felt hot, my face flushed. What was I nervous for? I was ready for anything to happen.

"It's gonna be fine". Elise who was sitting beside me noticed the horrified expression I had on my face. She patted my shoulder. I knew she was trying to calm me down. I closed my eyes and breathed in and out, trying to relax. It was getting louder and louder. Some of my classmates started to act up from the suspense. Whispers began about the room.

"It's a prank"

"Someone must be trying to play a trick on us".

"They gonna get in trouble soon, you'll see". I wish it were so.

I could feel Elise's hand gripping against my shoulder. She was expressionless. Looking up at the intercom speaker. I had no idea of what

3

was going on inside her head. Could she be thinking about the same thing?

"Hey". I asked her.

She turned back to look at me. "Funny, you'd think...I'm crazy if I were to say what was on my mind right now". Her face grew dark.

"I already know what you're thinking". She told me with a grin.

"Oh"? I whistled.

"And... If it actually comes out to be true then, we'll already have a plan".

She eased her grip on my shoulder and patted my head this time.

"We'resmarteh"? I asked her. She nodded back at me. I sighed. The intercom came on again, but this time all of us heard someone say "Help". It sounded no more like a silent whimper. Then it grew louder again with more force in their voice.

"HELP ME"! The voice shook us all. After that yell for help several noises started to come out of the intercom speaker. Sounds that shouldn't be heard by these people, sounds that shouldn't exist in this peaceful school.

"H... HELP ME... HELP ME PLEASE...SOMEONE"!! Aside those words, the sound of something crunching on bone. Consistently chewing. The cries grew shorter and quieter. Until nothing could be heard from the other side. Everyone settled down. Their stirring calmed.

"Maybe it was just a pra-". Then the loud clamouring came back for a second attack.

"AHHH"!! Intense cries coming from the intercom scared even me, down to my core. From that, the scream was the only thing that moved me. I got up from my desk. Unbuttoning my shirt, I breathed in and out. I'm prepared.

4

"Elise...take "that" out". She looked at me confused.

"What"? She asked me. My gaze was hard and stern, she knew what I was talking about, what was making her hesitate to take it out.

"We have to go now"! I shouted at her. She shook, she looked surprised. Though I can understand her. I've never once ever raised my voice at her. I almost feel bad about it but, during a time like this I have to.

She rummaged through her backpack looking for the paper. While she did that, I tried to stay calm as much as possible. I started to look around the classroom. I took notice that my classmates' eyes were on us. Studying our movements. Then one of the guys from our table grasped my hand. He asked me,

"What are you doing"? He was a big guy, with spiky hair like any other ordinary young man would have to look "Hip".

"What do you mean"? I looked at him straight faced.

"I mean...you guys look like you're gonna go somewhere".

"Yeah, we are". I told him. He jerked in his chair.

"What if...it's not a prank...it's too dangerous to go out there"! His grasp tightened. I could tell that he was really worried for me and Elise, but I can't let him worry over someone like me.

"It's gonna be fine, I... we know what we're doing". I wanted to give him one more smile before we left but, I just couldn't do it. I released my hand from his and walked over to the door.

"Okay, I got it. Let's go". Elise jogged over to me with my backpack. I looked over at the teacher who seemed reluctant for us to leave.

"Where are you girls going"!? He walked over to us. One thing I hate about the teachers in this school. Their way too nosy.

"None of your business". I said, with my back turned.

"You know you're not supposed to leave the classroom... when...until the principal allows you to".

"But he hasn't said anything has he. Besides...if we were to stay here any longer..." I didn't say anything else. If I were to give away anything surely, they would think I'm crazy or something.

"I'd hate to stay in a cramped-up classroom with a bunch of cowards". The teacher clicked his tongue. I snickered. It does feel a bit good. One would never get a chance like this.

"Oh, but I do have one last thing to say". I turned around to face the students in the class. I'll give out one more piece of advice, to you all. Hopefully you will understand and follow it.

"I do wish you all...the best of luck. But for whatever reason you hear anything else from that intercom". I pointed to the speaker.

"You cannot...and I repeat, you cannot leave this room". After I said this some of the students in the room started to giggle, as if I had told them a joke.

"What makes you think that we'll listen to you of all people"? You'll listen because I'm smarter than all of you.

"Um, sorry if this may seem rude but...who are you again"? I scratched my head in confusion.

Another thing about me, I have the habit of forgetting the people I meet. (More like, the people I don't care about). It's only a minor setback in my personality, but I guess that makes me who I am.

I glanced at the one-meter stick on the shelf of the white board and grabbed it. The teacher stepped back. Oh, don't worry if I was going to hurt a teacher it would have been far more embarrassing than being hit by a meter stick.

"Then, if you don't wanna listen to me...do you want to be in charge of this class"? I asked the guy. A jock, this guy was a jock. From what I could see in his appearance...he was a top-notch jock. A block head at that too. I can't say for certain that he was dumb. (He would occasionally score higher than meinthetests). Besides that, he was just plain stupid.

"Hey, have you ever watched people in movies fight with swords"? I asked him.

He nodded.

"Ever thought about using one"? I asked him. He shook his head.

"Would you...like to have a duel with me, it's a quickie though". Elise who was behind me tugged on my shirt. She pulled me to the side. "What do you think you're doing"? She looked pissed. Oh man, I hate getting her pissed.

"Hmm, having a quickie duel...what about it"? I grinned. She grinned back and punched my arm. It hurt.

"Make it quick, we don't have time for you to fool around". I poked her with glee and turned back to face the guy. I looked at the meter stick. Looked long enough for 2.

"Wanna fight me"? I asked him. He chuckled. So, did his friends. They also got up to pat the guy. Encouragement won't do anything for ya.

"Ready to get your butt whooped"! The guy said. (Who uses that line nowadays?)

"Sure". I smiled brightly. Holding out the meter stick, the guy looked at me confused.

"This should be suitable"! Using my knee, I threw the stick against it, splitting the meter stick into 2. I looked at the 2 pieces.

"Looks even enough yeah"? A few people in the classroom gasped in amazement. But I don't get it, shouldn't everyone be able to do something like this. I shrugged and handed the other piece to the guy.

"I wanna ask you something, Bro what's your name"? He looked angry.

"It's Anthony...you jerk".

"Whoa, no need to get foul mouth in here". I stood comfortably still with the other half of the stick in my right hand. He looked fierce. I'm sure that he thinks I'm weak...think again. Then we went into his ready stance. I laughed a bit inside. It seemed that he tried to replicate a samurai's stance. I'm sure he's watched a ton of those kinds a movie.

"Go easy on him Jade, he doesn't know what he's doing". Elise was leaning against the wall. Waiting for me.

I waved my hand at him, gesturing him over.

"Anthony, you can go all out but...I won't guarantee the safety of your arms or legs". He gave me the middle finger and charged at me. You're gonna tackle me or...

I took a step back, as he plunged for me I moved swiftly to the side dodging him. My back facing him. He took a second swing aiming for my head I blocked him with my hand. He stumbled against the white board. While he kept swinging at me like an idiot, I just kept dodging him, waiting for the perfect opportunity to strike.

"Stop dodging me"! He wailed at me.

"But I'm worried that you'll damage my face"! I giggled. His anger grew.

"K"! I stepped back took a deep breath in and aimed for his legs. I stabbed his legs on several different pressure points. Just the few where it would disable him from any further movement.

"Gah"! He fell to the ground. He looked so pitiful. Unable to move his legs. I put my hand to my mouth trying to hold back my laugh.

"Oh, stop been a cry baby you'll feel them again...in a couple of minutes". I bent down and picked up the other half of the meter stick. I tapped him on the head with the stick.

"Now are you gonna be a good little boy and listen to

me"? He nodded as he shook.

"Good, now then". I let out a big sigh and got up, throwing the sticks to the ground. I knew for sure that these won't be of any use to us for where we're going.

"Let's go already".

"Yeah". We headed out. I shut the door behind us and walked away.

"Do ya think they'll actually listen to you"? Elise asked me.

"Now, I just wanted to show off a little before we left". Elise gave me one of "those" looks. I see that she's still pissed huh.

"Eventually they'll wanna found out by themselves. Though it's unfortunate".

"Yeah". When I think about those people in the classroom. I feel sorry for them. But, it's their faults. Just the look of them you could tell that they wouldn't be able to withstand or stay sane for long.

"You know what I hate most about humanity". I crossed my arms. "What"?

"We're so blasted curious about things, no matter how many times someone tries to stop you from finding it out...you'll want to persevere. It won't last long. The imaginary barrier that I've set up".

"Imaginary barrier"? Elise looked at me confused.

"Yeah, it's gonna break soon, and once it's broken..." I looked up at the ceiling.

"And... Once it breaks"? Elise asked. "Chaos". Curiosity is the deadliest

thing on Earth. That's what I think. You

may think I'm silly for thinking this but. There are just some things that...

shouldn't be found out.

It's like what mom would say.

"Don't open a can full of worms".

"Why say that"?

"It's easy to open a can full of worms...but it's rather difficult to

close it back up".

"That's a rather odd saying".

"Yeah, and my mom's a rather odd woman". We both laughed at my

joke, but in all seriousness, I wish that all this scenario was just a big joke.

Chapter 2

As we walked down the wide darkened hallway. I asked Elise as   to where we should go first.

"Did ya forget already, wow Jade".

"What"? I looked at her confused.

"We planned that we'd first head to the sports dept. to go get the keys. Then get to the sports shed where all the equipment is". She pointed to the paper.

"Oh, right...sorry". She's being so bossy.

"Are you mad at me"? I looked at her I was pouting. She looked back at me with a stern looking face. Said nothing and continued to walk forward.

"I'll take that as a yes". I cleared my throat. The air had become rather heavy. Course I won't blame Elise for this feeling but, the whole school's atmosphere had changed in such short time.

"You feel it"? Elise spoke.

"Yeah". I said back. The hallway looked deserted; we found no trace of the hallway monitors walking about.

"They must have hurried to the speaker room".

"They're just doing their job but going there now won't change anything". I thought to myself, they must be dead.

"How unfortunate". I folded my arms around my head. But there's nothing we could do about that, it's too late. And I wouldn't want to stray from the plan. In all the silence, only the rough tapping of our shoes surfaced. My feet more specifically since I strut longer than Elise and I'm... heavier. I shook my head.

"Don't think about things like that in a time like this". I told myself.

"Think about what"? Elise asked me.

"Hmm"! I sprawled my arms out trying to stretch. I cracked my elbows.

"You're talking to yourself again right"? She gave me one of those looks again.

"And? What of it"? I crossed my arms again. Looking ahead.

"You need to stop doing that or else people will think you're a weirdo".

"I...am a weirdo already...I don't need you to tell me something like that Miss awkward".

She punched me again, walking a little faster than I was. I seemed to have pissed her off more than I should have.

"Elise...girl, I'm sorry. But if you get mad now, we'll be distracted about this. You need to stop getting angry so quickly".

She's got a short fuse; I know this from past events.

"Are we close to the sports department office"?

"Here". I looked above me, a sign which read: "Sports Dept. Office".

"Yay, we made it safe and sound". I cheered us on. Elise gave me another cold stare.

We walked into the office, I looked around first to check if anyone was around.

"Coast clear". Elise made her way into the room. We took our time, making sure not to make any loud noises. We wouldn't want anyone to find us in here without passes.

"Where should we look first"? I asked her.

"It should be in one of the desks". She walked over to the first desk that was closest to the door.

12

"This is...Mr. D's desk". The desk was filled with different files, several dog bobble heads, and a wrist watch.

"Man, never thought someone would have dog bobble heads on their desks".

"It's not that bad". Elise shuffled through the drawers.

"Huh, you would've thought they were locked". Elise held out a paper clip, which was bended so that the tip stuck out.

"No way, did you unlock it with that"?! She looked at me and nodded. "That actually works"?

"Only if you know what you're doing". She gave me the clip and told me to put it in the bag. Might need it in the future I suppose.

"Hey check if they actually keep marijuana in there or any drugs". [Chuckles]

"They wouldn't be stupid enough to ke-". Elise must have found something. She looked deeper into the drawer. She picked the object up and held it in the air.

"Are you kidding me"?

"Pfft"! I fell to my knees and started cracking up. I slammed my hand against the desk multiple times, while covering my mouth. My voice wanted to escape. It was too blasted funny I just couldn't help myself.

"The hecks wrong with this teacher, keeping this kind of thing in here". We actually found a small plastic bag containing a small amount of marijuana. And a pack of cigars. (The crappy kind, it's a real shame).

"I was joking, I never thought that they would actually keep something like that...ha ha, oh lord. I can't, that's too..." I couldn't breathe after laughing so much.

"Need some help there, getting up"? Elise held out her hand. I grabbed

13

onto it and slowly got up from my crouching position. My knees have gone numb. It's been a while since I've crouched down like that for a long time.

"Ow".

"Stop acting like an old fool you're not that old...not yet". Elise said.

"Ugh but, it hurts". I looked at her with pleading eyes.

"If you're thinking that I'm going to massage them for you, think again"! She pointed at me. We walked back into the hallway and made our way to the sports shed. Unlocking the shed, the room was filled with tons of equipment. Baseball bats, basketballs, tennis balls, rackets, cones, nets, soccer balls, etc. I walked over to the baseball bats.

"These will do fine". I grabbed one of the bats and swung it around the room.

"I'm surprised they're not wooden".

"The schools not that poor". She also picked up a bat.

"Should last us long enough to get out of here". I swung the bat a couple of times in the air. I made a sound effect with my mouth, as the ball hits against the bat.

"HOME RUN"!

"You know that you could never even hit one ball right"? Elise smirked.

"Have some faith eh"? The bat fell to my side. We made our way to the kitchen. It was odd. There was no trace of any people in the area. I thought this was pretty strange. During this period, you would have found a couple of the lunch ladies making food. (Rather, heating it up). Looking around we found no other usable weapons.

"No knives, huh"?

"It's too bad". I never would have guessed that they would use actual

14

knives in this school. I was fully aware that the food they make here isn't fresh. More like, shipped frozen and reheated in the oven or something. Aren't most schools like that.

"Wait, duck". Elise crouched down behind the open window which faced the lunchroom. She gestured me over and told me to be quiet. I crouched next to her. She pointed up. I poked my head up ever so slightly to get a glance.

"Look at em". I remembered it was lunch time. In an ordinary lunchroom there are about a couple hundred students. Maybe less I wasn't entirely sure.

"They seemed to have ignored it". Elise pointed to some of the students in their seats. They ate their lunches as if nothing ever happened.

"This feels strange".

"What does"? Elise asked me. I sat down and leaned against the wall holding onto the bat.

"No one...knows the truth". I gripped the bat.

"This scene. It's gonna get real ugly soon". Elise said. And she's right, with that many people in there it might just turn into a blood bath. So many people will get killed. And it just makes getting out of here a lot harder than it should be.

"We should go now, before someone spots us". "Y-yeah". We crawled through the door into the hallway once again. "The atmosphere...it's so heavy". It was hard for me to breath. I couldn't possibly be having an asthma attack could I?

"No, that's not it. It's not a physical thing". My heads all messed up.

"Elise, besides anything else. Did you get in touch with your family yet"? I asked Elise.

15

"She... Didn't an swert hephone. It's like all the phones stopped working. But I know they're all fine". She paused; her face was dark. I knew she was worried, but she can't let that distract her.

"What about you"?

"Hm". I swung the bat around gently. It made a whistling noise with each swing, the bat cutting through the air.

"I...Don't need to worry about my mom. Besides it's... impossible to kill her". Elise stopped walking all of a sudden, and looked at me with a disgusted expression. I looked back at her and smiled.

"W-what do you mean when you said, "It's impossible to kill her"? I spun around once and looked at Elise.

"It's exactly what I meant. No matter what you do that women will not die"! I spread my arms high in the air, trying to show amazement. Unfortunately, Elise thought differently.

"Saying something so morbid with that nonchalant look, the hecks wrong with you"?

"Oh? But it's true dude". She smacked the back of my head with force.

"Ow"! I rubbed the back of my head, when she hit's you it's gonna hurt...it's gonna throb for a good couple of hours, the woman's a blasted psycho. (Course she doesn't know this for I don't want to die at 17) "She trusts me, and I trust her. But I'm telling you right now, she won't die. I won't let death take her now". I paused and took in a deep breath. (This is when the heroin makes a grand speech in those heroic type anime's)

"I'm not gonna let her die nor will I allow you to. We planned this since the beginning, you and I are what's left or those who oppose fear and death. So, I need you to trust in me". I looked intensely into the dimmed

16

hallway. (Man I feel awesome)

"Kinda...sounds like you're proposing to me". My eyes grew wide, I was in shock.

"I...didn't mean it that way, you're the only on thinking that. Idiot". (Propose, what?) We stopped talking to each other for a while, that was what normal folks would call "An awkward situation". Walking down the large hallway I felt a sudden presence. I squinted my eyes down the hallway. Lurking in the darkness a figure appeared. It was limping, as my eyes focused you can see the figure. Its skin torn from the muscle and bone, blood splattered to the ground leaving a trail. With each step it took you could almost make out a cracking sound. It walked aimlessly around the hallway. Searching for pray I guess.

"Ja-". Before she could speak I pulled Elise around the corner of a wall.

"What"? I covered her mouth my hand.

"You have to be quiet". I whispered. She wanted to say something but her voice was muffled by my hand. I removed my hand.

"What is it"? She asked me in a hushed tone.

"There's one coming this way". Elise poked her head around the corner. Once she saw the figure she rushed right back behind the wall. Her body shook.

"Whoa". She gasped.

"Scary,yeah"?I grinned.

"What, what's with the grinning Jade"? She stuttered.

"It's started already". I crouched down with the bat in my hand.

"I call first dibs". I stared at it, the figure grumbled and groaned. Like a wild animal.

17

"C'mon get closer". I whispered under my breath. I tightened my grip on the bat. Getting ready to swing at it.

"C'mon just a bit more". Everything was quiet, for that brief moment I stopped breathing. The figure was only a few inches away from me. Elise grew restless next to me.

"Just kill the blasted thing". She shook her head, pounding it against the wall. Once the figure was close enough I rushed out from the corner positioning my bat. Jerking the bat behind me I swung it around hitting it. In impact the bat cracked through the figures skull. The bat went through like nothing. It didn't take much to smash its head out. Blood splattered all over the floor. Some ended up on the lockers. A dark red that didn't look human at all.

Chapter 3

Didn't take much to take you out, huh". I pulled out the bat from the things head.

"Um jade, you kinda got some on your cheek". Elise pointed to my left cheek. Which had a speckle of blood from the thing.

"Well now, luckily it didn't hit my eye or mouth". I took off my shirt to wipe the blood from my cheek.

"Yeah". Elise was still.

"You look so tense, ease up will ya"?

"Ease up? What if more of em come"! I gave her a small grin and chuckled.

"If more of them come, then I'll just have to..." I picked up the bat and hit it against one of the lockers creating a crater.

"Smash every last one of em into smithereens"! I laughed. I turned to look at Elise who I presumed would be amazed by me once again, she gave me a quick smile and punched my back.

"You're...an idiot alright".

"What"!? She started to laugh but with all the distraction I felt another presence. Suddenly one of those thing appeared behind Elise.

"Watch out"! With quick reaction time I threw my shirt at it covering its face.

"Whoa"! Elise ducked forward. I was about to attack it with the bat until something awesome happened.

"Sneaking up behind me..."! Elise leaped back, she jumped past it tugging on the sleeves of my shirt, and she used all her strength to pull the thing over her body, thrusting it down to the floor. It made a loud bang once it hit the floor. It struggled on the ground, using its hands to claw away the shirt. It coughed up blood, soaking the mouth are as tainting my shirt.

"Is a big no, no"! Elise grabbed her bat and cracked its skull, crushing the brain in the process.

"You sounded cheesy just then". I told her. She looked at me and laughed.

"Yeah I know". I looked down at the ground were the thing laid. No longer moving.

"That was a rather killer move, yeah"? I looked Elise who seemed satisfied with the situation.

"I've always wanted to use it, never thought the day would come". We both chuckled.

I stretched again, waving my hands in the air. I grunted when a popping noise came from my left shoulder. We stayed in that area in the hallway.

"At least no one's coming out, I wouldn't want to fight a hoard in this narrow hall way".

"Same". I started to hear clicking. The sound of doors being unlocked and opened. From upstairs we both heard screams.

"Curiosity...is a scary thing no"? I looked at Elise easing the bat on my shoulder.

She looked at me confused.

"We better, get moving now "They'll" be here soon".

"What"?! From the far end of the hallway behind us, a crowd formed. About 20 students even more started running down towards us.

"They're normal"? Elise said.

"No". Behind them you could clearly see unidentified figures in the darkness. These people were being chased by them. Screams could be heard, they echoed against the walls, sending slight shivers down my spine. I was scared yes but thrilled at the same time.

"C'mon". I started to run towards the stairs, Elise was right behind me. I jumped from the top of the stairs to the bottom, the impact numbed my legs for a brief second. It was painful but I continued to run. Course Elise took her time to run down the stairs making sure not to slip midway. Another flight downwards to the first floor. More people started to show up.

"These people are skeptics, they didn't believe meat first... now look at the mess they've created". Elise looked at me. I could only imagine what's going on in this building. People running wild in the hallways, trying to find a way out, pushing each other, losing trust. Many other things went through my mind.

"Look"! Elise pointed towards the main doors that led to the outside. I looked behind us. The same crowd still followed. Screaming. Since they found a way out should we,

"Should we lock them up in here"? I asked Elise.

"What are you talking about"?! She shouted.

"Think about it, if we were to let out this many people it'll spread faster".

"You're not thinking straight, why would you leave innocent people to die in here"!

"Innocent...."? We both looked at each other, I ignored the thought.

"Chaos". We pushed opened the door. The warm air touching my skin, the summer breeze felt good.

"I wish to cherish this warmth". I said.

"Me too". Thinking back on it, I never did like the summer heat. It would always be too hot in the summer around here, too hot to go outside. I would feel sluggish just reaching my hand out the window when I felt like it. The pool was also out of question, since it would be filled with too many people. Plus, pools are gross. (Do you know how many people go in there, they might have even peed). But there are some benefits from summer. On some days when the heat dies down in the afternoon, I would walk around the neighbourhood park. Get a tan. But what gets me each time is the midday's warm breeze. It was neither too hot nor too cold. It wasn't chilly either. It was absolutely perfect. I would want to stay outside until the sun went down. But now that this has happened I can no long cherish that moment. I cannot walk around.

We have to keep running and running, with no one else to trust but the people dearly close to us. We keep running until we find salvation.

"How are we gonna get out of here". I thought. We headed towards the parking lot.

"A car"? Elise looked at me strangely.

"Yeah...what's wrong about it"? I looked at her my eyebrows raised.

"I got a better idea than just a puny car". Elise smirked. She tugged onto my tank top and moved me over to where the buses were.

"A...bus"!? I was dumbstruck.

"Yeah, it's tougher than a car and it can hold more"! Elise giggled, I reached for my forehead covering it with the palm of my hand. A bus really. I sighed in frustration.

"Well, c'mon". She forced opened the doors. We jumped back in surprise when we found the bus's driver still in his seat.

22

"He's...not moving Jade".

"Yeah,I know".I reached over with the bat and poked him.I felt Elise flinch behind me. Oh, come on we don't have time for this.

"He's dead".

"Dead"!? Now, now Elise should you be scared of a dead human being when you've already killed something identical.

"I'll go on this side, you come up here with me. We're gonna push him out". I needed her help, this man was huge (And not to offend other huge people) but he was big indeed.

"Okay, on three".

"One...two...three"! We shoved the heavy man from his seat, he landed on the ground outside making a thud sound. I was out of breath.

"You...drive okay"? I told Elise. (Not that I can't drive but, it's for the best). She started the bus, while I looked around for any unwanted passengers.

"Clear"! The bus was in movement. As Elise closed the doors, I pressed my hands against the glass windows of the bus, watching those people scatter. I saw few being eaten already. These things weren't fast but they were pretty strong, since once the brain functions shut down there is no restraint for the strength they use. I couldn't possibly think of how they ended up this way,but I have a few theories.

Elise drove fast. Almost past 50 miles an hour.

"Turning left"! She screamed. I hung onto one of the chairs as she turned. The force was strong I didn't want to fall over. I'd bump my head for sure, and that wouldn't be good now would it. Getting farther and farther away from the school. I started to feel regret. I carefully walked to the front of the bus. I rubbed my head and sighed.

I was stressed out, I would have never thought that this day would come so quickly. And unnoticed.

"Hey, Elise"?

"Yeah"? She kept her eyes fixed on the road.

"What do you think happened, for this to..." I paused. Elise gave me a quick glance.

"You know, in those zombie movies...the cause would most likely be an outbreak of a certain virus, or maybe when they were testing new ways to cure cancer something went wrong, or in most cases there was that one bad burger and one thing led to another...now this will come to reality". I chuckled. She sounded sarcastic in a way when she told me this. But a few of those might be the reason.

"Well, whatever it is... there's really nothing we could do about it, only..."

"Run". Elise said.

"Yeah...and keep running". I looked at the blood covered bat behind me.

"Course we must fight right"? Elise grinned as she said this.

"That was in the plan". I patted her shoulder. We both laughed. At times like this I was glad that we were ready. Even when people thought that things like this would only occur in movies, I never stopped believing.

"We need to get to the junior high fast, to save the damsel in distress". I chuckled.

"I wouldn't really call her damsel". I paused.

"Then...she's just in distress"? I looked forward, my face a bit puzzled.

"Yup". How blunt. But all jokes aside, we needed to get there quick. Before those "things" get to her first.

"I imagine many of them are there, like a hoard of them...like, a load".
Elise sighed.

"Don't jinx it now"! Ah, there goes her accent. (It's so
funny) "I'm not just thinking about it".

"How bout ya sit yo fanny back in that seat, and shut yo trap. Do ya
wanna get in to an accident"?! She raged on, in her accent. (Up to this
point I have no idea what she's saying). I sat down.

"Thank ya. Blasted, can't I at least drive in peace and quiet"? She
mumbled curse words under her breath. I am, quite twisted...if getting her
pissed...makes me laugh aren't I

Chapter 4

As we approached the school, I shook in fear. The amount of those things were, scary. Probably most of the school had been infected already. Elise slowed the buses speed down.

"Don't get so close to the school, but just enough so that when we get out of there the bus will be close by". I leaned over her shoulder.

"Kay, its close enough let's go". I grabbed my bat and told Elise to open the doors.

"Take the keys with you". I said.

"I know"! I jumped down from the open doors. And looked around. The infected did not notice our arrival. Maybe, "Hey Elise"?

"Yeah".

"Remember that one Anime we watched"?

"The one with all the explicit scenes, and boob action"? She said with a straight face.

I held back my laugh, so as to not alert the infected.

"Yes, with all that Elise".

We stopped walking for a bit. I pointed to one of the infected with the bat.

"Wanna try something"? She looked at me confused. I looked around and found a small rock. Just big enough to make a loud noise.

"W-what are you doing"? Elise looked at me.

"Just an experiment". I walked forward towards the scattered bodies.

There was many of them all over the place. Infections lik this sure do

spread fast don't they. Just like a zombie movie. I looked behind me, Elise looked concerned. I nodded to her telling her every things going to be fine. But how should I know that, if this "Experiment" fails I'm in trouble. I got close to a few of the infected. Gripping both the bat and the rock. Taking a closer look they looked horrid. If the infection just started today, why did their skin peel? Rotting bodies that moved in daylight and at night. Their eyes white...empty. Moaning as if they're in pain. Though I doubt they could feel anymore. Trying to catch my breath, I breathed heavily. I was nervous, scared, I'm practically risking my life. But I mustn't let it show on my face. It's not as if I'm trying to impress anyone. Maybe it's my pride. Under my breath,

"To heck with it". I stepped back and threw the rock far from where I was standing. It knocked against a car door. I waited for what felt like forever, they began to move. But not towards me, but to where the rock fell. Maybe 20 of them began walking towards the noise.

I waited for them to be far enough. And I waved at Elise to walk over to me. Once she was near me, I rested my head on her shoulder and sighed.

"I guess, the experiment went well".

"I was about to mess myself" She giggled lightly and patted my head.

"Alright, let's go. But quietly the rock is the distraction". We jogged over to the school silently.

"Are the doors locked"? I asked Elise.

"They usually lock themselves once it's shut. So may-". I smashed the bat against the window of the door, reaching for the lock. The glass fell to the ground.

"What are you doing"! She shouted at me in a whisper.

"I don't think they noticed...come on let's go". I heard her sigh behind me.

"I'm surprised the alarm didn't go off". Elise looked around.

"Well, this is an old school wouldn't be surprised the alarm system broke". Thehallwaywasdarkerthanourhighschools.Muchnarrowertoo.

"I hate having to come back here". I said.

"Yeah, same here". I grimaced. Then I noticed that there weren't any infected walking around.

"Maybe most of the students got out using the other doors, or emergency exit's".

"Which explains why there isn't anything here...at least for now. Let's keep moving". We looked around in each classroom. Found a couple of infected. In one of the hallways, the light above us flickered. The perfect setting for a horror flick.

"It's kinda spooky in here". Elise said as she stepped closer to me. "Well, it's been like that forever. I don't remember having a "sunshine and rainbows" type junior high life". "Haha, sunshine and rainbows". Elise chuckled.

"So, where do we look for Nika"?

"I'm not sure, I don't know which class she was in". Nika was Elise's little sister. She's got her own little personality. Me and her got a long pretty well. She was easy to understand.

"D-do ya think she's okay"? Elise asked.

"Yeah I'm sure she's fine...after all I did train her". The secret behind our strength. Acouple of years agoI studied Taek won do, plus some military combat training. Though I'm pretty good with a gun, I specialize more in swords. Especially a Katana. A Japanese sword.

I only own two pairs of swords. Don't ask where I got it from I wouldn't tell anyone that. Since long ago, I was taken for a weak child. Because of my asthma it was a bit hard to move around. But during the training I grew stronger and running got a lot easier. But, I'd rather appear weak just to heart he stupid comments coming from my friends and teachers.

"Do you want to check the kitchen"? Elise asked me.

"Yeah, let's hope they have some useful weapons". Passing through more rooms filled with infected, we got to the lunch room.

"They seemed to have spawned here". I said. As I gazed at the dead bodies that roamed the room. A few were teachers the rest were students. I remember the students here to be very short.

Not to sound mean but that's what I remember the last time I was here.

"You know, I don't remember being that short back then". I said looking at the short infected bodies.

"That's because kids nowadays are shorties. Well, at least half of them are".

"You got that right". We entered the kitchen. We looked quietly throughout the kitchen for any usable weapons. I rummaged through a box full of cooking utensils.

"Hey I found something I think you'll like". I walked over to her and saw that she was holding two kitchen knives. I skipped over grinning widely.

"Perfect, achef's knife. But, are there more than two"? I asked her. "Why? Do you need two knives"? This girl. Doesn't she know? "You don't know"? I asked her, I took both knives from her. And started to swing them around.

"What"? She asked me, while backing away from me.

"I mean, fighting with two knives, twice the power. It's what makes the person using the weapon more awesome". I kept grinning at her, she looked at me confused and sighed.

"What"? I asked her.

"Nothing" She said after she sighed again. She then took another knife to take along with her.

"So you're gonna use two after all huh". I said to her.

"I wanna look awesome". She said with her back turned. I chuckled. It's nice to make a few jokes now and then to ease the tension in the atmosphere. But right after the jokes comes the truth. I was still thinkingabout theinfection.How did itreallystart? Iwanted to know more about it, maybe more than Elise did. But thinking about that now would only distract me.

"The infected huh"? I said. Elise slowed her pace down and walked beside me.

"What"? She asked.

"You know, Calling them infected...Don't you wanna give 'em a code name or something. Like they do in that show the walking dead"?

She looked at me with cold eyes.

"We don't really have time for that Jade". She shook her head sternly. She started to walk ahead of me.

"No really, let's call them something different". She ignored me for a brief while, until she turned around and said,

"Bodies then". She said with a straight face. I looked at her while grinning but my eyes weren't smiling.

"B...Bodies". I said. She nodded her head.

"Bodies". She repeated. We stopped walking for a while. I needed time to think this over. Was she really serious about that name or she was

31

only joking "Walkers sound so much cooler, but you couldn't come up with something even better than that? Bodies you say". I detested her idea of calling them "Bodies". It's like their no different than normal humans. She raised one of her knifes and held it up pointing to me neck.

"You wanted a code name for them, I gave you one. You don't like it come up with one yourself". She said coldly.

I Gasped. (Dramatically of course)

"Okay, okay we'll use it then". I back away slowly.

"Good, let's go then. We're never gonna find Nika at this rate.

And just standing here doesn't help the least bit". We continued our walk around the school. More infected started to show up once we got closer to the main gym.

"Is it just me or we're beginning to get more popular with the infected"? We started running.

Elise looked worried. She doesn't have to be, I'm sure Nikas alright. She's tougher than she looks.

"Two of them ahead near the main doors"! I shouted. No use being quiet anymore.

"I'll leave them to you"! She shouted ahead of me. I grinned.

I started to sprint. Faster. I took out both knives. Placing them against my lips.

"Don't fail me". I whispered under my breath. Once I got closer I jerked back and stabbed the infected's head dragging the blade across the skull, revealing bits of the brain. I took back the knife. Blood splattered against the walls. I whistled in excitement.

"They sure sharpened this to perfection"! Elise was right behind me. Smashing the day lights out of one of them with a bat. I went for another only this time I used the bat. Knocking both its legs out it fell to the ground. Growling it tried to get up again. I clicked my tongue and crushed its head with the bat. Few more of them started to appear in front of me. One tried to grab my arm, I pushed it against the wall stabbing it in the eye with the knife. I cocked my head to the side, like in those old time killing action movies the blood sprayed out. I must have hit a blood vessel or something.

"Be careful not to get it anywhere near your eyes or mouth Jade"! Elise ran ahead of me.

"You don't have to tell me that"! The knife was stuck to the wall.

"Not now". I took out the second knife, another one appeared behind me. I lifted my leg kicking it back. Once it was down I tried to focus on the knife.

Getting a better grip on the stuck knife I pulled it out with ease. I turned around. The one I had kicked down tried getting back up.

"Oh, no you don't". I threw the knife pinning its hand against the floor. It groaned. I walked closer to it. Getting a better view of it.

"Wow, you sure are ugly". I giggled. I raised the bat above its head. The only line going around inside my headwas: Finishhim!

Since I tend to say that a lot when I used to play video games. Ignoring it I smashed its head into the ground. Staining the gray carpet with dark blood.

I took a chance to get myself together, and ran after Elise. She was standing next to themain doors. She looked atme with anger in her eyes.

"You're Slow"! She said. Then that other word came up inside my head.

"FATALITY". I said in an even deeper toned voice than usual. I looked

33

at her and smiled. She smiled back, and hit me in the head. Ignoring my cries of pain she pointed to the center of the gym. Inside you could see many of them.

Chapter 5

T hey roamed about. "There must be 30 of 'em here". Elise leaning against the wall.

If you're wondering as to why we are so carefree is because, since the infected only react to loud noises all we have to do is stay quiet.

One of them passed beside me, but it didn't attack. Even so I'm prepared for anything to happen.

"So...where do you think she is"? I asked her.

"She's in here alright, but she's hiding". I looked at her. Her face was tense.

"Where"? I asked her.

"The only place left to hide in". She said. Then she pointed to the supply closet next to the stage.

I stayed silent for a while.

"Why would she be in there"? I asked.

"Course to hide, stupid". I scratched my head.

"So, what's the plan"? I asked again. Elise stayed silent for a while.

"We...get in there quickly, get out with Nika, then exit". Was all she said?

"Uh..Huh". I looked at her with confusion.

"What's the matter"? She asked me.

"Or... like, we can throw something in the distance to distract them, get Nika, and then exit". Elise knocked her head against the wall.

"It's the same blasted thing, Jade"! She roared (In a whisper).

"But I explained it better. You gotta be more specific". She coughed and punched my arm.

"So, what's the distraction this time"? She asked. I thought about it for a while. Then I thought of the most brilliant of all ideas. I chuckled and beckoned Elise to come near. I then whispered in her ear.

"Me". I said. She looked at me, astonished. She stayed wide eyed for a couple of seconds.

"W-w-w-wha"!? She asked in a loud voice. I tried to cover her mouth with my hand. She struggled. Her arms flailing in the air.

After a while she calmed down and looked at me with soulless eyes.

"What? It'll be fine. Trust me". I said. She shook her head. I smiled and took my hand away. She stood silently. I then patted her head. "Trust me". I knew she didn't like this plan but, just for a bit let me be the main heroin Elise.

"On 3". She nodded. Gripping both knives to her sides. I jogged over to the end of the hallway on the other side of the gym. I was facing out looking beyond the sea of undead. I waved over at Elise who was positioned on the opposite side. I took one deep breath in and exhaled heavily.

I raised my hand up. I started the countdown.

"1..." Elise tensed up. Facing the closet.

"2..." In that moment everything stopped. My chest was tight.

My heart beating against it, faster and faster. Beating harder creating a lump in my throat. I breathed in.

"3..."! I Shouted. I saw Elise sprint for the supply closet. The bodies began to move towards me. And the ones behind me as well. Everything, with my own two eyes...everything seemed as if it was in slow motion. Elise's legs slowly stepping against the wooden floor. I also began to move away from theroom.

"Come at me you undead mongrels"! The Dead Sea began to rush in towards me. (It looks rather deep) I thought. Small droplet's of sweat started to fall from my face. It glistened against the dim lights. I looked back. More...more of them rushed after me. Limping or even crawling with so few limbs attached, they came after me. Gasping for human flesh.

"Elise"! I was at the end of the other hallway. I drew farther and farther away from the gym. If I were to shout loud enough maybe she would hear me.

"ELISE! IF YOU CAN HEAR ME, MEET ME BEHIND THE SCHOOL...NEAR THE SPORTS FEILD". I waited for a while. No answer. I kept running the first floor of the building started to swarm with the undead.

"This isn't looking good". I ran faster, with my lungs trying to supply oxygen. It became harder for me to breath. Was I going past my limit? I was gasping for breath my throat began to burn. A metallic taste in my mouth with each huff. As I got to the second floor. More of them showed up. I dashed beside them heading for the closest classroom. Locking the door behind me. I scanned the room for any remaining bodies. I ran to the window. And looked down, since this was the second floor it wasn't that high up. I got on top of the small book shelf. The sudden banging of the locked door shook me. I looked back, and they started pounding on it.

One of them managed to break through the glass. Arms went flying between the broken windows.

"Impatient are we". I chuckled. I took the metal bat and smashed the window in front of me. I hit it again with more force, only cracking the first layer.

"This isn't gonna work is it...Oh"! I grabbed a lone backpack next to the desk beside me. Weighing it, it seemed heavy enough.

"Sorry about this...but it's an emergency"! I threw the back pack against the window shattering it entirely. I whistled at the amount of power it had, to break the window.

"The heck did they put in that? Bricks... no encyclopedia books". Sounds like something Elise would do. I adjusted myself on the window seal and jumped, landing hard on my feet. Any normal person without the right muscle could damage their ankles. As for me the impact felt like nothing. I dashed across the fresh cut grassleavingtrailsofdetachedgrasstoblowinthewind. Ilooked around for Elise and Nika. A few of the infected roamed behind me, seems they haven't notice me from the noise yet.

"Guys"? Trying to catch my breath. I gazed at the bright sun.

"Jesus, if it was gonna be this sunny I should have put on some sun screen".

I placed both my hands on my hips.

"Does it really matter, you're already tanned out". Nika showed up behind me, she hooked her arm around mine, leaning her head on top of my shoulder. I chuckled and looked at Elise. She gave me the death eye. Yeah,I know we don't really have any time for this.

I placed my hand on top of her a uburn brown hair and pet tedit.

"Are you okay"? I asked.

"Yeah". She said using her high pitched voice. Something she'd usually do from time to time.

"How'd you get into that situation"? She looked up at me and smiled. "I have my ways". She said. You know the thing I'm mostly jealous about are her and Elise's eye colors. It's like looking into a clear glass

38

bowl filled with aquamarine sea water. Almost like water colors. Orange, blue, and green. Mixing together to create something beautiful. I'm really jealous.

"Idiots". I whispered under my breath.

In a world full of mess, why am I worried over something so trivial...? I'm dumb.

The sun's warm rays burned against my skin, over time it began to turn red.

"You okay Jade? You're uh, looking a little bit red there". Elise poked my arm, the stinging sensation made me twitch.

"Wow". When she removed her finger, a pale mark was left in the spot. I glanced over at her. She bit her lip and grinned motioning her finger to poke me again in a different spot.

"Stop it, whatever you're doing". I grabbed her hand and jerked it away.

"Okay,okay"! She snickered. When she woulddo this hernose would scrunch up revealing lines on her nose bridge. We continued to make our way to the school bus. I scanned the area around us, nothing in sight.

"I guess that distraction from inside the school managed to get their attention". I felt like I just did something awesome. Since it was my plan from the start, I feel pretty smitten.

"Stop grinning like that with your bazonga bosom shot out". I gasped. Placing my hand on my chest I knew I was acting a bit dramatically but it was the only way I knew how to react. Plus I was wearing a tank...it wasn't showing that much.

"How dare you! I'm actually very proud of these girls. And what the heck is a "Bazonga" From which dictionary did you pull that one out of"?

39

She looked at me coldly.

"A new word I just made up" she said in a monotoned voice,

"From my book of insults just created for Jade". She finished bluntly.

Before I had anytime to say anything back she dashed inside the bus.

"When a zombie grabs you by the hair one day...I'm gonna leave you there". I said in a hushed tone. I made my way into the bus and settle down on one of the seats in the very front. I looked over at Nika who was standing in the back.

"Where to next"? Elise shouted from the driver's seat.

"Read the paper stupid, that's the reason why we made it in the first place". I rolled my eyes in annoyance.

"Why are you so irritated"? Nika sat next to me on the seat beside me. "I dunno". I said, as I yawned I felt a cold stare on me. Elise was looking back at me.

"Start the blasted bus already"! I yelled back at her kicking the back of the seat in front of me. Her head shot forward. The bus began to move.

"Is it that time of the month again"? Nika said bluntly. My eyes grew wide, I turned my head slowly to the side facing her. Shocked at her sudden question.

"No..." I sighed. I slouched in my seat. Nika moved herself closer to me.

"Then what's wrong"? She asked using her high pitched voice. I paused and finally said,

"It's because I'm Bipolar". I smirked, crossing my arms against my chest as I relaxed.

There was silence for a while. I bet they were both shocked by my answer.

Nika was staring blankly at me.

"What"? I asked. She placed her hand on my shoulder and squeezed it. "Bipolarity is a serious condition, don't make little of it". Her face was serious. I raised both my brows.

"It's true though..." I closed my eyes in frustration.

"Really"? Her voice rang through my ear.

"Yes...really". I was actually very tired. That's why I'm so irritated. Plus it's hot out, I hated this intense heat wave. The indoors where it's nice and cool is the place for me.

"Weren't we headed to Walmart"? I said with a long sigh. If I remember correctly, we were supposed to head over to our homes and check for our parents where around.

Elise glanced at the rear view mirror in front of her. Looking at me she grinned.

"Yup, But before that we should head over to your place first". I looked over at Nika who was fast asleep on the seat next to me.

"Why is she so carefree in this type of situation"? I grumbled under my breath. "Should I wake her up"?

"No, let her sleep for a bit". Elise sighed heavily. We were all tired after just one day of this chaos. But, sleeping is an unimaginable thing right now. I'm actually quite afraid to sleep, because once I close my eyes all I see is darkness. I'm afraid to rest because of those "Things" out there. Chasing after us, chasing after the living. And If I dream, I wouldn't be able to wake up from it. I looked out the window, the sun started to hide itself behind gray clouds.

"Looks like it's gonna rain". I knocked my head against the window.

"Yeah".

41

I soon got tired of sitting down and got up to get our bag. Sitting back down I unzipped it and checked the contents.

"Did you bring you're cell phone Elise"? I shouted from the back seat.

"Yeah, but it's running out of battery".

"Once we get to my apartment wanna charge it for a while"? I asked.

Elise turned her head slowly.

"Yeah, I wanna check mytumblr and Instagram". She said this sarcastically. "#killingzonbieslikeapro". In the same tone. (Hash tag) I heard her giggle, it was quiet. Making jokes like this, it was fun. Sometimes these type of things make me forget about what's really going on. I grabbed my cellphone and checked the battery.

"Mines still fully charged". Since I don't go on those applications as much as she does. She's a freakin psycho. Aftera while we finally arrived at my apartment. I leaned over Nika shaking her shoulders gently.

"C'mon let's go". I said in a still voice. She winced.

"Mkay". Rubbing her eyes, she struggled to get up from the seat.

"Did you sleep well"? I pinched her cheek. She nodded.

Before we got off I made sure to grab the keys, wouldn't want anyone to drive away with our ride.

"You have everything, weapons"? We talked to each other quietly. Making sure not to cause any disturbances. Being here, isn't the right location for a hoard. The area around our neighborhood was small.There was a large intersection in the center.Trees covered most of the apartments. By my bedroom window a tree branch blocked the view. I was happy about that. Reason was is that our place faces the sun, in the morning it was show through a blind me once I enter the living room.

"Be cautious. Don't let your guard down". I clutched the iron bat in my right hand tightly. Securing two kitchen knives against my belt.

"Let's go". We made our way across the street. Nothing in sight.

"I don't see any Bodies walking around". God I still feel a bit weird using that plain word as a nickname for those things. I told Elise to wait outside the apartment as a look out. Nika was stationed in the back near the alleyway. I jogged up the stairs to the first floor. It was dark. It had nothing to do with the lighting. But the atmosphere. I noticed that the door to the apartment across from us was open. The door had been ripped off right from the hinges. I wanted say I felt calm about this whole situation but I would be lying. I wanted to investigate it further, but the voice inside my head was telling me no. Ignoring it I headed inside my apartment. Everything seemed normal, nothing was misplaced.

"Don't think anyone cleared this place out yet". I walked around the corner into thekitchen. My eyes grew wide, the inside was completely covered in blood. The back door wide open. I took in a deep breath. The stench was horrid. Looking down at the floor, you could make out slight scratch marks.

"Struggle". I whispered under my breath. Some one must have tried to escape from one of those things but eventually got caught.

I placed my hand against the door. Gliding it against the splintered wood. Red hand marks covered it completely it trailed off into the neighbor's apartment. I didn't want to know. I didn't want to see. Without looking back I closed the door and locked it with the chain. How stupid, why did I lock it.

"It's meaningless". I walked over to my mom's room. Once I opened the door, the scent of cinnamon filled the room. I glanced over at the scented bamboo sticks my mom had put up a week ago. The room was clean, everything in order. And then I felt a warm liquid trickle down my left cheek. It dropped down onto my bottom lip.

"Salty". Man, I shouldn't be crying. This is pathetic. Every time I think about it I start crying.

"I need to stop, I don't want them to see me like this". I hope you're safe mom.

Chapter 6

Nika 2 hours before the spread Sitting on my arse for such a long   time, nearly broke me. It was like, if I had to sit much longer I'd fall asleep and I wouldn't be able to feel it the next time I get up. And trust me the feeling isn't pleasant.

Ms. K spent half of the class time explaining to us about the importance of safety when handling the needles. When I mean needles I mean like, sewing needles. I've already gotten down the basics and what not. Heck I can even make my own clothing now. All we ever do in this class is sew together pillows and plush toys. And some of the others works are...pretty half- assed. At least some of us are trying to pass the class. It's like the easiest class besides the cooking part of the subject. Pretty sure my siste couldn't even pass that class. She sucks at it.

Right now, I'm working on a dog plush toy, I haven't done something like that before.

Minding my own business, I noticed that the room had gone totally silent. Like, one of those "awkward silence" type moments. Except the mood wask in daintense. I was so engrossed with what I was doing, it took me a couple of seconds to find that my teacher Ms. K, was sprawled on the floor. I didn't even hear a thud when her body dropped to the floor. Not with all the sewing machines making noise. We all just sat there, for a couple of minutes. And all I heard was the loud ticking of the clock behind me. I got a bit nervous and worried. Then one of my classmates got up from his seat and walked over to Ms. K. I realized that my hands were shaking. But why, she'd just fainted. Fromexhaustion?

But, she seemed fine not too long ago. Ranting on about sewing. This and that.

Not one of us even thought about going outside to ask for help. We just froze. It's like one of those moments when you experience fear. Sometimes you scream, you face it, and sometimes you just stay still. Unable to move. Unable to think. I got curious and walked over. Once I got closer she didn't look normal. Her skin turned a pale gray. And her arms were covered in bruises. They might have showed up just now, because before those weren't there are all.

Her head was on its right side, she must had hit head first. There was blood oozing from the bottom of her head. It was dark, and thick. I thought normal blood was supposed to be brighter. It was almost black. I looked up at the guy that was beside her.

"D-did you see her fall"? I asked. My voice was shaky.

"I wanted to ask her a question and just like that-she landed on the ground in a second". He said. I knelt down beside her, observing. Hesitant, I placed my fingers close to her nose. She wasn't breathing. Then I felt her wrist for a pulse. Also nothing. She can't be...dead.

"Is...She dead"? He asked, his face scrunched up with worry.

"I-I don't know". I leaned in to open her eyes. When I did, I could have sworn my heart stopped for nearly a second. She had such cold-dead eyes. Both heavily blood shot. It was like gazing into the eyes of a dead fish.

I turned my attention to the others behind me. At some point one of them started to cry. If one person starts to freak out then the others will follow after. It got noisy. Their screams pierced my ears. Let's see: there's a probably dead person lying on the floor in front of me, about 15 screaming shiznit heads behind me, and I'm about to freak out too. Losing my patience, I got up and smacked both my hands on the table.

"Shut up, I can't think with you all shouting in my ears". The room went quiet. I sighed in frustration, doing that it I was finally able to shut them up for the moment.

I turned my attention back to Ms. K. I noticed that her mouth started to open and close. I leaned in closer, which obviously wasn't a very good idea. My nervousness grew worse. My heart pounded against my chest, I could hear it. After a couple of minutes, I could have sworn her arm twitched. Then again, and again.

It slowly rose from the ground reaching for something. Her eyes cold staring ahead, she was looking at me. I stared at her, as her hand grew closer to my foot, I wanted to move, but it was like I was glued to the floor. I felt the hairs on the back of my neck stand straight up when her hand finally collapsed onto my foot.

She groaned and hissed. It was almost inhuman like. Then it started, everyone started to panic.

"G-Go and get another teacher"! One of the students shouted from behind me. I heard the door close. It was muffled. I was too focused on what was going on in front of me. The noises got louder. And she began to move. Closer and closer she crawled towards me. I backed up against one of the tables. Why wouldn't my legs move, I could just stand up and get up on the table. But they didn't listen to my demands. One of the guys jerked my arm up and tried to get me to stand. But it wasn't possible. My legs were weak.

"C'mon get up Nika"! He shouted. It was right in my ear too.

I shook my head and punched both my legs. I could feel the pain but it wasn't enough to wake them. I used both my arms to push myself up using the table. After a couple of seconds, the numbing in my legs began to fade.

I stood above her, looking down at this "thing". I wanted to think of this as a prank, like one of those candid camera things.

You know, those T.V shows where they try to scare the mess out of random people and capture it on camera...just so the people at home watching get a good laugh out of it. I shouldn't be talking though, I'm one of those people. It's freakin hilarious.

This wasn't normal though, if she was wearing make-up then it's too real. And why would they want to scare us.

I felt a tug on my shoe, her hand was grasping at it. She held onto me tightly, pulling me closer to her...mouth?

Blood dripped from the corner of her mouth. I shook her hand loose. But she was persistent. This time she got up from the floor, and tried walking.

"Ms. K"? I called out her name...she didn't answer back. I did it again, nothing. She just groaned. Stretching both her arms at me. Then I realized. This just might be a silly guess but.

"She's turned into a zombie". The guy next to me chuckled nervously. "N-No way, that's impossible. Zombies only exist in h-horror movies". She's showing similar signs of the undead. Ya' know. Dead eyes, starting to rot skin, dark blood oozing from everywhere. I'm both scared and surprised. I knew this day was gonna come. Well it's not like I wanted it to. Knowing Elise this would get her ecstatic.

"Well I guess it doesn't just happen in movies". I heard the door slam open in the next room. Loud footsteps growing farther and farther away.

Looks like they're having the same problem.

I stepped back again, her arm swung across me. I almost forgot about this one. I can't really say that she's still my teacher. Just another lifeless corpse. Instead this corpse is trying to tear off my limbs and eat them. I bumped into one of my classmates, she was shivering.

She looked at me with confusion and fear. Tears streaming down her cheeks. I told her to get out of here quickly. The room was almost empty. It was almost silent, if it weren't for the hair raising screams coming from outside the hallway.Someone burst open the door yelling, cursing all kinds of things.

"They're...eating each other out there! What the hecks going on, is this some sort of prank". This guy, so clueless got dragged away by another one of those things. I remained totally calm somehow.

"I thought the same thing". Before the corpse got any closer to me, I grabbed one of the knitting needles on the table and struck it into the things right eye. Its hand clasping my wrist it stood there for a while, then it fell to the ground with a heavy thud. She wasn't moving any more. Blood gushed out from where the needle was. A dark puddle emerged from underneath herhead. The guy next to me gagged and vomited on the floor. He hunched over trying to hide the sight.

"How...why did you just...kill her"?! He tottered over, wiping his mouth.

"I had no choice, but to". I said coldly. "If I were to hesitate she could have eaten my insides". He looked at me in anger. I grinned.

"I was taught to act this way towards zomb zombs, if this situation were to ever happen". There really is no helping it. You .have to KILL them. There's no other way, unless some crack pot quack doctor decides to make a vaccine, which looking at the progress of the infection in person...I doubt that they could create such a thing. It would take at least 4-7 years. I mean you have to study the virus, then experiment on people who were not yet infected.

That's just too much responsibility for one person.

"If you're not willing to kill a couple of people to stay alive... then you're pretty much done for. Well I wouldn't technically call these things human anymore, so killing them shouldn't bother anyone, right"? I picked up a couple of knitting needles and placed the munder my belt strap. I'll find suitable weapons soon enough.

Hm I've forgotten this dude's name. What was it again...Matt I think.

I looked back at him and smiled.

"Ya' coming or not"? I leaned against the table.

"Where"? He twitched.

"Weare gonna run and most likely kill a couple of those things out there to escape". I made a running motion with my legs and stabbed the air rapidly with a knitting needle. I puckered my lips when I did this. Bet I looked pretty funny.

"You're sick"! He slammed his hand a top the table. He did it pretty hard, bet it hurt.

"Then I guess that makes "her" the same". He gritted his teeth in disgust. "Course her personality is just as messed up, ya' know"?

Ah, I'm boasting...that's the proper term right?

We both heard a thud at the door, it was soft. The pounding became louder. A hand flew right through the glass window.

Clawing against the door, then two arms. Flailing in the air. It was almost funny, like foam pool noodles wobbling up and down, side to side.

I giggled loudly. Before we knew it a hoard of them busted down the door, ripped it right off its hinges. They came pouring in it was horrifyingly exciting. Good thing they were slow arse zombies, I hate runners.

"Get on top of the table if you don't wanna turn into a zombie meal"! I jumped up, and looked into the crowd, for an opening.

"Run on 3". He looked at me worried, what does he not trust me or something?

I held up my hands for the countdown, obviously I couldn't help myself from skipping 1 and 2.

"3"! I ran down to the table's edge, jumping from the ledge I landed on one to soften the fall. Knitting needles in both hands I struck those around me, aiming for the head. Blood spurt from every direction. Some of it got on my clothes, I made sure to cover my mouth with cloth. I looked over head to see if that wuss of a man followed my instructions. Of course he didn't, I found this jackass on the ground, crying in pain. Getting eaten alive by these undead mongrels.

"This is what you get for not listening to me". I created a small gap that led into the hallway. I was running out of knitting needles. So I just immobilized the rest by taking out they're legs.

Kicking below the knee, the shin. One by one they fell to the ground. I pushed my way towards the open doorway. My body ran into the side wall of the hallway. Bumping my shoulder.

"Ugh, that's gonna leave a big fat bruise". The hallways were surprisingly desolate. I would have imagined countless zombies crawling around looking for fresh meat. They must have walked out of this area. They can tell by scent...or was it sound, I'm not really sure.

I peeked around the corner and found 2 of those things, walking aimlessly. One of them bumped into a wall and just kept hitting it. I wanted to laugh but apparently that would be too loud and it would make them notice me. I tip-toed across, I need to be sneaky.

"Like a shadow in the night". I whispered under my breath. I'm treating this like it's a video game. A zombie video game. Only, once you die...you stay dead. I found a couple of people they ran towards me. Their faces red, clothes bloodied, bodies trembling.

"Nika, you're okay"! I don't recognize this person's face.

Hm, I'm pretty well known around this school. Sorry mystery person but,

"I'm glad to see a few people who are not...you know, dead". I smiled pulling down the cloth from my mouth.

They nodded, and asked whether or not I've seen more people around. I told them that from were I came from. My section had already been taken out. I only saw a few of those things but, not too many to be of any threat. I then said to them that they should get out of the school and seek help. They've probably got the S.W.A.T or military scattered in all of the areas that have been reported.

"Don't you want to come with us"? They asked.

"I need to go find my sister at another school. It's a high school, farther from here but. I'll make it there somehow". They looked worried but I shrugged them off and walked right back into the fight. There are exactly 7 exits in the whole school. Some of them have a security lock, which locks from the inside. I guess they don't want anyone ditching school. Like a prison. It was all too quiet.

An average person wouldn't be able to keep it together in this type of situation. Somewhere in the distance I heard screaming.

"Everyone's going bat crazy now". I coughed, skimming the wallbeside mewith my hand. When I turned the corner, I spotted 4 of those things. Getting a closer look, I recognized the first 2.

One was my history teacher and the other was science. I smirked,

"Well, isn't this awfully convenient". I slowly raised my arm, knitting needle in both. I sprinted down the hall.

"This is for giving me a load of homework to do over spring break"! Jabbing the needle into his head, he collapsed to the ground. Groaning, his arms flailed around looking for me. I smashed his skull in with my foot. I remember seeing something like that in movies a lot.

I turned my attention to the other teacher and pounced forward, knocking her down. She struggled to get up, I didn't have enough time to pin her with the needles so I smashed her head against the wall.

"And that'sfor taking mycell phoneaway"! ‹It's a distraction'.

Distraction my arse. Once I got rid of the other two I continued walking. I got to the main gym. It was empty. I rushed over to the other side to lock the doors on the opposite side. As I was doing this. The ground beneath my feet began to shake. I wasn't just imagining it. I quickly turned around and those things had already started for the door.

"Man". Did they smell me or something? Was I the only one left alive? These doors wouldn't hold forever. I knew that. They only lasted for 10 minutes. On both ends the doors were knocked down.

They came rushing in like starved animals that were kept unfed for a long time. I ran with what little energy I had in me to the nearest supply closet. Locking the door behind me. I crouched down between a basket of soccer balls and some cones. Iwas in one heck of a situation. If I would have known they were gonna rush in like that I could have made it to the head office to unlock the doors.

"I'm so stupid". My body began to tremble a bit. I told myself to calm down. I told myself to hold out, because I knew that my sister and Jade were gonna come and save me from this crazy mess. I'll keep quiet and stay completely still. If I were to move and bump into something. Then for sure I'd be totally fudged.

Chapter 7

I rubbed my eyesfuriously.Usingmy tank towipeaway anylingering   drops.

"Get it together" I slapped my hands against my cheeks. Closing the door behind me I walked into my room. I knelt down in front of the closet placing my head against the cooldoor.

"It's important so, give me permission". I opened the sliding door slowly. Turning on the light, I pushed away boxes that kept

"That" away from my mom's sight. There was a small hook in the wall, I pulled on it opening a small latch.

Inside the wall was a small opening. Kind of like a secret space.

I just made this a year ago, just to keep all my important things away from mom. I took out a long silver colored box which said: FRAGILE pasted all over it. I lifted the top off setting it on the floor.

I took out two katanas from the box. The first one had cherry blossom sprinted on the sheath, with a small yarn voo doo doll that I had gotten from a coin machine tied around it. But my favorite was the other katana. It was my very first one that I had received from a friend from Osaka, Japan. I met him when I went there for vacation. It's a long story.

The sheath was in black. I've never used it so it's not chipped and the paints still clean. I've never used any of them so I've waited until the day I could actually use them. In the past my mom was opposed of the idea of me have owning these "dangerous" weapons. Soon Iwasableto convinceherthatwhen thetime comes only then will I use it. For a while they were only used as a decoration.

"This is one of those times...and you're not here so I'll be taking these". I tied a support belt behind my back. Call it a place holder for the katanas. These weigh around 20 pounds each.

But enough about that. I placed the katanas in the holder. I walked around the room for a bit. I was gonna leave all of this behind, I knew that I was never coming back. The dust would pile beneath the bed, in the little crevasses, which I don't clean so well says my mom. I sniffed back a tear and headed out the door. When I got to the living room a faint scent filled the air.

It was rotten and musty. I poked my head out the only open window beside me, and was alarmed to find three of those things approaching from the left side. They must have loitered nearby they were coming from an alleyway. I rushed down the stairs heading towards the back of the building. I spotted Nika hiding behind a trash bin. She noticed me and signaled me to stay where I was. It was late in the afternoon, which casted shadows in the inner corners of the apartment, I leaned back against a dark wall and hid.

There were only three of them, both I and Nika knew that we could easily dispose of them without causing a ruckus. They got closer, they're limbs detached from their original places. This scene would have frightened my mom to high heaven,shewasn't used to gory things like I was. I would usually have to watch the movie with her since she was such a baby.

I slowly raised my arm and took out one of the katanas behind me. It made a slight clicking sound as I dislodged it from the sheath. Gripping it tightly in my hand, I looked to Nika for conformation. She waved and thumbed up at me, grinning giddily. I nodded and rose from the darkness, walking slowly towards the Bodies. The one in the middle flinched as my foot made a noise against the dry grass. Without hesitation, I sliced through the things rotten flesh making a clean cut across the neck. I stepped back as the head fell to the ground, its body next to it, dark liquid began to spray out of where its head used to be. Leaving a puddle of blackness on the dry earth.

I sprinted forward cutting off the legs of the second Body. It didn't feel fair for me to kill these things off by myself so I kicked up dirt towards Nika, who was still kneeling behind the trash bin.

She giggled lightly, and got up, kitchen knife in her left hand.

Although I gotta say, Nikas method of "Finishing off" left the poor thing limbless. I sneered at her with both amusement and disgust. It wiggled on the ground, no arms nor legs. Only its head attached. It wasn't a pretty sight I must confess. I was surprised to see Nika walking awayfrom it. I guess shewanted it to stay like that, it kinda looked like a defense less baby looking for its mother.

I wiped the sweat forming at the top of my forehead, and struck it's skull with the tip of my katana.

Nika and Elise were standing by a tree. Elise's foot propped up behind leaning against it. Nika was fiddling with her hair, retying the braid. I wiped the blade of the katana against my shorts, removing the blood before it would dry and never come off. Elise threw her hand in the air and waved me over. I looked around making sure that there were no more of those things nearby.

"So, Nika told me you guys ran into a little bit of trouble back there". Her voice deep, serious but oddly excited.

"Yeah". I placed the katana back behind me, Elise eying the two blades strapped against my back. She bobbed her head forward gesturing towards my new toys.

"You weren't kiddin when you said you had real katanas in your apartment". I smiled widely. Pretty sure that my dimples were now visible.

"I know I lie a lot but..." She grinned then snickered loudly.

"Unfortunately, Ihavenoguns or sniper rifles in mypossession".

I placed my hand on my hip.

"I wouldn't be surprised if you did, but I'm happy you don't".

Yeah, I'm not old enough to own a gun, and my mom's too... goody-goody to have one either. Ever since they made that law about only the police and whatever-No one's supposed to own any guns in this area. It makes sense though, at least it put to rest for some of those neighborhood shootings and stuff. I didn't care much about stuff like that, so all of it disappeared into the back of my head, lost in the black hole of what I call mybrain.

"If we stumbled upon an S.W.A.T car of police station, I'll remember to look for one". I placed my hand across my stomach and bowed. "Only the best for Mistress Elise". I said in a soft British accent. Trying to copy a butler tending to his master's needs.

"I am most thankful to you, Sebastian". A very stereotypical name for a butler. Elise said this in the same manner. I peeked up at Nika who was trying to hold in a laugh. And what she did was very smart because, that girl's laugh could alert all of those things to our location. Like a siren. When we were done joking around. We walked down the road towards Elise and Nikas house.

It was only a two blocks away from my place. We often hung out together at they're place. Well, perhaps 'hang out' wasn't the best way to describe what we would do. Normally, Elise would sit on the couch and be on her phone, I would be on the opposite couch either drawing or watching T.V,and Nika would sit beside me. Sometimes lay down next to Elise. So, I guess that's how we would normally hangout. It sounds boring, but it made me happy.

When we got to the house, everything seemed normal. It didn't appear to be disturbed. The door was still securely locked like it always was. The windows weren't broken. I felt a little angered by the fact that my apartment had been torn apart, while their home seems as if nothing bad has happened. Elise sighed in relief, and Nika was probably in her room looking for things. I walked over to the back door, and found it locked and in place as well. They must have not gotten to this place yet. They're parents were both busy so that comforting. They were aways from here, maybe they were takeninby the military before shizn it hit the fan completely.

I placed my hand against the wall, and sighed heavily.

"Calm down, they're safe...they're all safe. Their parents and my mom are somewhere safe". A lump began to form in my throat.

Again this feeling, washed over me. I wanted to cry. The worry swept over me like a dark cloud. I hated these feelings most of all.

The anxiety, the stress. The very feeling that makes me tremble and want to curl up in a ball and forget it all for a while. This rarely happens...
I force it out of me. Make it go away. I punched the wall in front of me, again and again. I might have punched the wall at least 20 times before I could finally clear my head. Elise popped up behind me, her facial expression dim. I cleared my throat making sure the lump was gone. And spun around to look at her.

"You okay, what was that thumping"? She was scratching the dried paint off the door way.

"Nothing really, just trying to...calm myself down". She was silent then said,

"If punching a while is one of your calming exorcises then proceed with caution, don't do it too much, to the point that you're knuckles could bleed". She pointed to my hand, I examined the spot. They had already started to turn purple. I bruised it a little I think.

"I brought some medical cloth I found in the nurse's station at the school, I'll just wrap it up and it'll be as good as knew". I fumbled around inside the back pack until I found the cloth. Slowly wrapping it around my left hand, securing it with one of those pins they put on the cloth. I flexed my fingers and wiggled them towards Elise's direction. She widened her eyes and tapped the wooden door way.

"If you say so". She clicked her tongue and looked around.

"I'll be looking for things in my room, could you keep an eye out down here"? She looked down at my bandaged hand and up at me. I chuckled and walked past her, patting herhead.

"Only the important things alright? I'll hollerif I see anything".

I took my place and every now and then peeked out between the window curtains. I only saw a few of them walking nearby, but too far for them to be a threat.

I glanced at the clock above the door way,

"Already, 6:30 pm"? I scratched the back of my head. We were sitting in the living room. Nika on the floor eating a Nutrigrain bar she found in the food pantry. Elise was looking over our plan on the table. She used a small lamp to light the space around her, so as to not attract any unwanted attention. I played with my necklace. Which hung low around my neck against the top of my stomach. A silver cross, I dangled it in front of me. Swinging sideways. I usually wore it to school or going somewhere that involved vehicles. I wasn't one for churches or hyped up on that whole religious thing, but I felt safe with it. I made myself comfortable on a small chair which might have come from the early Victorian age.

It was petite yet subtle to sit in, the floral designs caught my attention the first time I laid eyes on it. I found it adorably charming.

My katanas were placed against the chair on the floor. I wanted to nap a bit before continuing our journey back into "Madness".

I extended both my legs out, slumping in the chair crossing them every other couple of minutes. We sat in silence for a good 10 minutes until Elise slapped both her hands on the table, making the room shake a little. I twitched trying to get out of the chair as smoothly as possible, knowing that my joints had relaxed a little too much making them crack and pop with each movement into standing position. I bent down to touch my toes and up bending back cracking it. I twisted my body sideways before confirming that it was okay to move around freely. Nika finished her third Nutrigrain bar, and sat cross legged on the floor looking at Elise.

"So, we rested here for a while. Now it's time we move on to the next location". She said this so formally I wanted to gag. She sounded like a freakin squad commander telling his team our next assignment. "We'll need a car for that". I messaged the back of my neck. Half yawning as I said this.

"Then we'll get one, once we go out". She nodded towards Nika, and folded the paper into a neat little box, placing it into a small pocket on the back pack, zipping it closed. I groaned in pain, seems my necks gone stiff from that earlier position I was in.

I blame the way my spine worked. I had scoliosis, my spine wasn't completely straight. It would curve slightly slumping my back and ruining my posture in the process. I got it from my mom. It wasn't that bad, it just hurt sometimes to stand up straight. I had to do that a few times for multiple different reasons. Pretty sure that when I grow old I'll have a hump.

I secured the holder behind me and placed the katanas into their slots. I laced up my boots tying it around then into a tight knot. Nika had gotten a few small sharp knives from the kitchen, which she placed under her belt. Elise was by the door, the metal baseball bat poking from the behind her. She crossed her arms against her chest and huffed,

"So, I saw maybe 4 or 6 of them out there, they haven't noticed us yet. We could both choose a car and run for it, or..." She looked at us, I could see the maliciousness in her eyes.

"Or, we could kick their arses, obliterating the threat...taking our sweet time picking out a suitable car". She said the last few words slowly, letting the' sweet' and' suitable' pass through her O shaped lips, emphasizing the 'S's longer than it should be. Still, I smirked with amusement.

"I like the second one". I licked my lips by habit.

"Same here". Nika said, her voice in that mouse like state. We looked at each other, then Elise opened the door, leaving its lightly a jar. She eased her hand outward, other on the knob.

"Let's go".

Chapter 8

We raced across the lawn. As the Bodies got closer wesplit up   and got rid of the lot, as many in the area. When I was finished on my side, literally both my katanas had been drenched in that black blood. I wiped it off on my shorts. Then slowly placed them back in their holders. When we got back together Elise was crouching down next to Nika. I told them to pick out a car, but I didn't mean a monster.

"Really"? I huffed placing my hands on my hips. Parked in front of me was a beautiful black H3 Mid-size SUV. It looked almost too conveniently placed. Especially in this area of the neighborhood.

"How the heck did you find this"? I walked around the vehicle, looking up and down. I need to savor this moment. I mean, when would be the next time I'd get to ride in this thing? I grinned giddily. Elise glanced up at me, giving me a wink.

"You like it? Whoever drove this car...is a total boss". Nika sprung up and jogged around to the driver's side. Elise patted the hood heavily.

"Though, unfortunately the only way were gonna get inside this is to-" Before Elise could finish her sentence, Nika leaned back and smashed the driver's side window with a baseball bat.

The shards scattered across the cement. The alarm went off putting all of us on high alert. I spun myself around.

"Gosh Nika! You know that's gonna attract them". Elise hurriedly opened one of the passenger seat doors and shoved Nika inside. She winced when her elbow made a heavy impact on the cup holder. "Get inside Jade"! She shouted from across the car.

"Did you hot wire it yet"? I asked. I started to get uneasy. Thecar alarm didn't silence until after a couple of minutes. Elise wasalready ducked down underneath the wheel, fiddling around withthe wires. She was still, and calm. Although her expression wore composure I could see the sweat dribbling down her temple. Her lips quivered, she whispered acuss and the car roared with power.

She sat back in her seat and placed both her hands on the wheel. I chuckled and turned my attention towards the window beside me.

My eyes grew widely when those things started to appear one by one out of every street corner. With each step sent shivers down my spine. They walked slowly. Their muscles visible, limbs missing. They paced towards us. I shifted in my seat. I clenched my jaw, massaging my knees. Elise turned towards me and smiled.

"I've always wanted to do this". I twitched, as she put the car in drive stomping on the accelerator. The forced pushed me back against the seat. I heard Nika stumble about in the seat behind me. Her foot poked out a top the arm rest.

"This is why you always need to put on a seatbelt". Elise tapped the steering wheel. Before I knew it they flew from every direction. One of them crashed against my side of the window.

Elise turned as harp left corner heading towards the mainroad.

I held onto the handle above me. I'd forgotten about how reckless she was at driving, since she only got her license a couple weeks ago. I went for my cross necklace. Holding it tightly against my chest.

"Lord, please grant me protection...I might not die from those things today". Elise took her eyes off the road and glanced at me.

"Aw, c'mon that's rude". She smirked as she made another sharp left.

I braced myself against the car door. Nika was still rolling around behind me. Poor child might end up with a few broken bones from this. We drove past many other cars that were headed in a different direction.

"Hey, turn on the radio". Nika squeaked, she leaned between our seats pressing lightly on the radio button. The first thing that came out of speakers were the only people I didn't really agree with.

"Oo, One D...fascinating". I grumbled and switched to the news.

"Reports have been coming in from every heavily populated towns in the state. Officials have noticed; a high alert to all citizens in the following sections..." I lifted up my legs and wrapped my arms around them. "We have confirmed that these occurrences have been reported in other states since yesterday morning. The estimated total of deaths so far...are steadily rising. Officials have not yet found the source of these deaths".

Nika started to kick theback of myseat. She seemedso carefree most of the time. Sometimes I don't understand her. "These people just don't want to admit that we're in the middle of a zombie apocalypses". She hummed.

They've only told us about the epidemic or tragic illness these people have been through. Right from the very beginning we all knew that something like this was gonna happen. It all started when that new vaccine came out during the start of spring. One that would help people with allergies and would be more advanced that the average summer vaccine. After all the recent sicknesses that have been popping up, doctors and medical university professors have come to get her to make this so called 'UltimateVaccine'.

Yeah sure, they've successfully tested it on animals or whatever they use, it still doesn't mean that it will work positively on the human body. It was after all a tested drug. Thank god I didn't get that thing injected in me. I'd hate to learn the consequences of an alien toxin swimming about in my blood stream.

I've had enough as is. Some waited for the summer flu shots other well, they weren't so patient. Then all of a sudden...boom!

All that mambo jumbo about the almighty drug sank down to the very bottom of the ratings. All those sorry people went through the pain and suffering for nothing. It didn't change anything, instead it broke down their immune systems. Slowly draining the strength in their bodies and weakening it. Like cancer, except it might have been more deadly.

"Stupid experimental drug. Those Idiot for brain doctors had no idea what they were putting themselves into". Elise bit her lip staring dead ahead at the open road. I would think that we were the only ones heading towards the danger. Most cars went the opposite direction. Trying to get out of town as soon as possible.

Not like they could go anywhere. The government hasn't issued a secured safe location as of yet. Of course they're only priority is the one person that runs this country and others that govern it.

The citizens come after. Sure they might have sent in the military but, something like this it's too late to stop. Like every other epidemic, it'll spread until every living being in the entire world is consumed by its madness.

I've been told before that I think negatively. I usually do it unconsciously, and it's unintentional but I can't blame myself for thinking like this...especially in this case. I opened the window and stretched my arm out. Moving my hand up and down, feeling the winds current like a wave.

"How long until we reach our destination"? I asked.

"Not long, about 10 more minutes". Elise gripped the wheel.

"I'd like the avoid meeting anyone...unnecessary while were there". She said.

"What do you mean"? I turned.

"What I mean is, anyone that could compromise our form. We have a plan and I don't want to involve anyone else". She said sternly. I've seen Elise serious...but this was a little unexpected of her.

"So basically, we can't make any friends or rather allies". Ieyed her curiously.

"MH. It's just...we can't trust anyone. You know the deal, there's always those kinds of people when situations like this occur.

I don't want to make any more enemies we've already got ‹those' things out there I don't need any more reasons to kill".

She turned right into a parking lot. Setting the car close to the store. Again we were a bit surrounded by those things out there. I leaned my elbow against the bottom of the window. I sighed.

"That means I can't get a boyfriend, huh"? I made a duck face as I glanced at Elise. She was leaning against the wheel. Nika giggled behind.

"Well...that all depends on if he can handle being with a psychopath then, it's totally fine with me". I punched her arm. I'll take that much sarcasm I know what she really means. I got out of the car closing it slowly, striking a pose in front of the store.

"Let's head inside then".

Chapter 9

Elise hopped out of the car, Nika behind her. As we walked closer to the front of the store. I questioned something "Hey Elise...Are we gonna leave this black beauty out in the open"? She crossed her arms and sighed looking at the car up and down.

"Then, where should we put it? Unless we find the loading dock in the back of the building...we can keep it locked up". She jabbed the air with her thumb, pointing towards the building.

"Firstly, we must clear the area as much as we can, if you find any survivors bring them together we'll talk about what position they have in our group".

Me and Nika looked at each other and snickered. Elise jumped in surprise.

"W-what"? She stuttered. Nika gave her an udgeand made her way to the doors.

"Oh, you know..." I patted her shoulder. She paused. The expression on her face was priceless. I chuckled. Me and Nika waited for her near the doors. They slid open automatically.

"Looks like the powers still workin' fine". Elise huffed beside me.

"Eventually it'll shutoff. I'd give it a few weeks.The generators would run out of fuel by then". Nika spoke in a whisper poking her head between the open doorways. I leaned against the wall.

While both Nika and Elise checked the area around us. I glanced over my shoulder, just a couple of Bodies here and there. They wouldn't go after us unless we did anything too loudly.

"Can we get this over with, the longer we wait here the more my skin will fry from the sun". The flesh around my arms started to turn a brightred. Don't supposed I could apply sun screen once we get inside. Maybe it'll be too late for that. I sighed with impatience.

"Alright, we stay together until I say so..." We all nodded. We all walked in. I glanced around, no one insight. I would assume they all left in a hurry. Just imagining hundreds of people rushing out between these automatic doors. It'd be just like black Friday.

So many bodies pressed against one another, probably tripping over each other. I thought I smelled something metallic in the air.

I doubt that Elise and Nika haven't noticed yet. The shelves were a mess. A pile of canned dog food (Once a towering pyramid) spilled over scattering the floor. I walked over to the cosmetics isle. Holding my self against the tendency to grab EVERYTHING.

Even now I think that I should re-apply my make-up. I looked at myself in the little mirror that hung on one of the shelves.

"Ugh, the eye shadows fading". I'm someone who really just, loves make-up. Honestly, I only use it to hide all the blemishes among other crap on my face. Without it...I would feel naked.

Because you know, most men only like sexy or beautiful women. I shook my head, leaving that thought aside. Nimbly, I grabbed a small bottle of liquid concealer and a stick of 'Bubbly peach' colored lip gloss. Might as well take 'em. It's not like I'm gonna get arrested for stealing, the cops got their hands busy with 'other' things. I roamed around. Looking up each isle.

I found Nika in the crafting isle. Flipping through rainbow colored crafting paper. I could see that she was having fun. While all this scenario is going down, I guess shede serves a little freedom. The rest of the storeis silent. Peaceful even, nothing but the light tapping of my short healed combat boots. I slung my backpack onto my shoulder, tightening the straps so that they don't slip. I check the food isle.

Almost everything was taken. Even the frozenfood.

"Oh, god...oh god no"! I rush over to the next isle. My boots squeak to a halt when my eyes set on the most horrific scene.

Among the jars that were left of peanut butter, marmalade, and jelly my limbs slacken at the empty shelf. Why? Even during the apocalypse why do people have to be such arseholes?

"No good, picky sh-". I stomped the ground in frustration. Alright I know it's silly of me to be freaking out about plain old Nutella.

Heck! Plain old Nutella my arse. Do I even have to say it? Nutella is life. Nutella makes the world go round, not money or...

whatever makes the god blasted world spin. I pinch the bridge of my nose slowly moving up toward the temples of my head. This is giv-ing me a headache and I have no clue why. I hear heavy footsteps, before I can grab hold of my katanas Elise waves a steady hand at me. I sigh, and sheath the swords back in place.

"Hey, what'd you find"? I ask trying to sound nonchalant. She narrows her eyes and crosses her arms.

"Nothing. They took most of the food but there's enough clean clothesandothernecessities". Shewalkedtowardsme. When she got to my side I hooked my arm around her shoulders and gave them a squeeze. She turned her head and looked at me, her brows grew together puckering her lips, and she looked at me as if I was some estranged animal locked behind unbendable bars.

"What...are you doing"? I ignored her question and leaned against her, placing myhead on her bonny shoulder. With a sigh I said what was troubling me.

"They...took all the chocolate gold". Inudged my head towards the empty shelf. She stilled against me. Then she wiggled loose and took a step closer to the shelf.

"I know, I know just how you feel Elise. It's unfortunate but we have to be stron-". Before I could finish my sentence, she jabs me in the stomach with here l bow. I bend forward wrapping my arms around my waist. Coughing dryly.

"W-what did you...do that for". I struggle with the words. As the coughing subsides I take a look at Elise, and she's scowling.

Tapping her foot with impatience.

"D'really have to be so dramatic? It's just Nutella Jade, It ain't gonna kill ya if you don't have any". She turned on her heal and walked away. I stood in shock. The one person who so openly screams to the world that her stomach is an endless pit just waiting for more food to be pulled towards it. Grumbling, I rubbed my stomach looked at the shelf once more and sluggishly walked away.

We must have spent a good 3 hours searching each isle. Finding more shelves disheveled and cleared. At one point I found Elise snacking on a bag of Doritos... specifically the cheddar cheese kind.I couldn't walk away or say anything. I just stood there while she devoured the contents inside plastic bag. It might have been a full bag three minutes ago, but from seeing her tip the bag up and shake the last bits of dorito crumbs into her mouth...the poor thing wouldn't have lasted two minutes the second her sights set on it. It. Was. A full bag. Might have been the last bag. The least she could have done was to save some for us.

"Excuse me miss, you gonna pay for that or am I gonna have to call the cops"? I said in a deeper voice. I must remind myself to drink some water, it's a bit scruffy. She burped quickly and crumbled the plastic bag in her hand tossing it to the floor. She turned to me and grinned.

You could almost see the evidence on one corner of her mouth. I blink slowly at her.

"You know...saving food does wonders during times such as these". I said with the wave of my hand. A slight British accent accompanying the sentence. She stood tall (Taller) jutting her chin out.

"First come, first serve". She said flatly. I clicked my tongue at her and side stepped playfully to the next isle. I heard her laugh after I turned the corner. Suddenly, a low pitched ringing wailed from the speakers suspended high up onto the ceiling.

"Attention...attention Walmart shopper's. May I request persons: Elise and Jade to the main office" A pause then the sound of a bottle popping open "I got surprise for both y'all, so get your chunkyass's up here".

Both Elise and I made our way up the stairs, which we found at the back of the store behind a security door. Wehad to wait a couple minutes for Nika to open it manually from her position. Once inside, I took in my surroundings. A compact room, glass windows surround the space. Covered by sand colored blinds. Several desks fill the room, and knick-knacks over flow them. Nika was sitting down on a rolling recliner I didn't notice the bottle of beer in her hand until it was too late. I leaned against the door frame as Elise went into full attack mode.

"What the heck do you think you're doin"? Elise snags the bottle from Nikas hand, the fizzy liquid inside sloshes out, dripping onto the floor. It's a Sam Adams...interesting choice.

"Give that back to me"! Nika pushes the recliner against the wall, it barely misses Elise.

"You're a dumb fool if you think I'm gonna give this back to you". Ah, this is another one of their day to day fights. And over a simple bottle of beer. I unclipped the back and front straps of the holder. Letting it drop to the floor quietly. I wouldn't want to interrupt. I took the chance to get comfortable by sitting cross legged on the gray carpeted floor.

"I deserve this Blasted! I have every right to drink this Stupid beer". Nika slammed her hand against the desk top making some of the objects on it topple over.

"No you don't, what if we have to run at any moment and you're not sober enough to escape"? Elise's face was turning bright red now.Even though thesubject of their bickering involves alcohol I'm quite amused by it.

"For god sakes Elise, It's not like I'm gonna get drunk right this moment. D'you really think I'm that stupid? It's just a bottle of beer, if I would have known you were gonna be a biatch about it I should have tossed the whole blasted pack out in the trash.

Will that satisfy you"?

Alright may be now I should intervene. I mean it's getting a little dangerous. Anymore argument and this might conflict all our plans.

It'll put them at odds and they'll never cooperate with each other.

I'm gonna have to get up and stop this huh...

I grunted and rummaged through the back pack. I took out a piece of paper from a spiral notebook and crumpled it into a ball.

I took aim and threw it right between the two of them. Making sure they notice the random white ball smack lightly against the window. They both quieted down, looked at the ball for a second, then turned slightly towards me. Elise was still holding the beer bottle.*Must be lukewarm now...sucks.*

"Alright you two, I've allowed you both to yell at each other for some time now but, I think that's enough" I cleared my throat before continuing on. "I'd like to consider Nikas opinion on the matter.Beer: consuming it during times such as these... I'll allow".I crossed my arms knowing that when I do this my bosom like to push up...unfortunately waving to the world of their glorious existence. *God, just stop*

"What do you mean you consider her opinion"? Elise growled at me.

"What I *mean*, is that who would care? None of the laws that once existed here exist now. Personally I'd love to take a shot of some tequila but, I choose not to because I would like to stay focused during these times. Now will you two please shut the heck up"?

They both focused on me, for a short while until Elise sighed and gave up. The bottle hovered over the piles of neat paperwork stacked high on the desk. At first I wondered if she was going to spill the rest of the liquid onto. Then, she thrust the beer bottle in my direction.

"Take it and toss it out". She said firmly. Her vivid green forest eyes burning (Literally) holes straight through me.

"What do you want to me to do with the rest of the alcohol"?

I asked, taking the warm bottle out of her grasp.

"Just make some Molotov's from half and the other for refuel". She straightened herself and stalked out the door. I took a glance at Nika who was otherwise very solemn. *Just give them a couple minutes to cool down, don't involve yourself in their arguments Jade* "You wanna help me with the Molotov's"? I asked Nika in my 'not-so-creepy-but-friendly' tone. Shelooked atmeand grinned.

"Naw, I think I'm just gonna scout from here. Oh yeah..." She lowered herself down and rummaged through the bottom drawer of the desk, she skipped over and placed a small plastic square in my hand. I looked at it closer, you could see the green, red, and yellow buttons taking up most of the square piece.

"What's this for"? I asked her.

"That my dear Watson, is the dock remote for the back". Her voiced sounded higher than usual, but I won't mention that to Elise.

"Great, we can put the truck inside". She spun around and dropped in the recliner.

"I've also got eyes on the outside..." She nodded towards the blue painted door in the far corner of the room. "Security system and camera's on all corners of the building, one in back, a couple more in front and of course ten inside". She then gave me the keys to the blue door. When I got inside, the room was filled with atleast 20 small video screens and a work desk. I sat down on a folding chair and played around with the video screens. Taking note that, in all of them you could see nothing but Bodies. There were more than the last time we got here. I shivered in wardly, no amount of killing those things will make the terror I feel go away. Appearing in and out of the camera view,my skin began to prickle, and the hairs on the back of my neck stood up. Thankful for the blue door separating me from Nika, I'd hate to show how weak I could become. I flexed my hands above the keyboard. Calm down, you're okay, just *calm down, in and out, you're fine* I took a shaky breath in and slouched into the chair. I stayed there for as long as I could, forcing my hands to stop trembling. After about an hour of looking over the surveillance feed, I stuck with a plan for the truck. *I've got to go over this with Elise, see if this works for her* I cleared my throat and got up from the chair. I shut the door behind me and tossed the keys to Nika, she caught them without even looking up. We've all trained ourselves to be flexibly alert, it's become a habit for all of us. Even my mom can catch things without me telling her to.

"Are there any walkie-talkies or comms"? I leaned my hip against the desk.

"Mm, second drawer to the left, there are four talkies". She was distracted by something in front of her. I looked over her shoulder; she was reading one of those magazines. Where she got it from, is the main question.

"What...the heck are you reading"?

"Ah, I found it rolled and snugged behind a drawer. Bet that person is missin' this thing pretty badly... I mean look". She flipped to a page that showed one girl on all fours; wearing something that resembled a bathing suit, crossed with bejewels. And that was all. I choked on my spit and slapped the mag shut.

"You really...shouldn't be looking at that, you're sisters gonna kill you and me for even finding it". She looked up at me, her face contorted, her lips twisted in an odd angle.

"Pshh, she ain't gonna care. Besides, it's only curiosity right"? I really have no comment for that.

"Nika. Get your arseupand monitor the survcams". I snatched up the magazine and tossed it across the room. Before I could make it out of the room, I felt something tap the back of my neck. A crumpled paper ball rolled between my legs.

"You and Elise are a bunch of ugly faced fun suc-". I grabbed my katanas from the floor and closed the door behind me, hooking the holder straps on my shoulder and walked down the stairs.

Elise was in the food isle...again. Only this time she was snacking on a box of chocolate chip brownies. It's a good thing that some food was left on the shelves, enough for all three of us to last for a month. I made sure that we locked the front doors and stacked a few car tires in front of them. It wasn't hard getting the truck inside. We waited out until the back and front were clear. Nika was on the cameras, Elise was the driver and I was sort of like the distraction. I sliced through a few of them, the roar of the trucks engine was loud enough to pull more of those things our way. *I took care of them mind you, most of them didn't even have any legs so it was easy-peasy* Thankfully the loading dock was large enough for the truck. We then, filled it with two 24 waterpacks, granolabars, cannedfoods, some spare clothes, and a first aid kit. We'd be set if the time came for that. For now, we can relax, at least that's what I hopped for.

Chapter 10

Y ou're gonna break a bone or worse"! I shouted from across the isle. This idea was definitely, absolutely dumb. Nika and Elise where both in mountain bikes on the other side of the store.

I'm not sure whose idea it was but, who's ever it was must be some sort of undiagnosed retard.

"Its fine, it's fine! Just wave the signal flag already". Nika shrieked.

"C'mon, Jade"! Elise made a sound which was supposedly the rumblings of an engine. I shook my head, this was idiotic!

"Fine"! I grabbed the make shift race flag (which was made from some checkered cloth and a decorative bamboostick) I stood firm, towards the end of the store,

"Ready"!?I shouted, myvoiced echoedaround theopen space. *I'm gonna regret this...*

"GO"! I swung the flag downwards, letting the tip, tap lightly against the polished floor. And they were off, Nika was ahead for a few seconds, then Elise rushed forward, the tires squeaking with each peddle thrust. When they got closer, I took a step back. Depending on how fast they were going I would not like my toes to be crushed, No thank you "Put those long legs to good use Elise"! I chuckled when she growled past me. They both screeched to a halt, the tires marking black smudges on the floor. I waved the flag once more to finish off the race, I was too distracted to tell who won.

"So"? Nika was panting beside me, sweat glistened on her forehead. I shuffled in place.

"Who won"? Elise was putting her bike away, grunting while she placed it back on the bike rack.

"You know what, I'm not really sure". Dropping the flag on the floor, I shrugged at them both, I found their expressions funny, too funny. So much so, that I wanted to laugh in both their faces about how ridiculous they looked. With their eyes slightly closed, and their lips puckered like a fish, how could a person not,

"I think I won". Nika sauntered to my side and hooked an arm around mine. She looked at me, fluttering here ye lashes. Shethen leaned in and slipped something into my hand. I felt the rough edges of paper and stilled. *Oh, she can't be serious.*

"Nika..." She looked up at me and gave me one of those "whatever is the matter officer" looks.

"Keep the change". She whispered into my ear. Good lord, what the heck is wrong with this child.

"You...cannot be serious right now". I wiggled loosed from her hold and held up the crinkled five dollar bill in the air. She just did it...

"Nika..." I sighed.

"All you gotta do is scream, "I DECLARE NIKA THE WINNER"! I blinked slowly at her, and heard Elise tsk behind me.

"She gave you money right"? She asked, holding out her hand. I gave her the green bill.

"Where'd you find that"? I asked Nika. She was spinning in place, jabbing the hair with her fingers.

"In one of the registers in front". She spun around until she tired herself out.

"Is that all you found"? Elise stepped up beside, she crossed her arms.

I glanced over and found that she was scowling again.

Don't fight

"Yeah, I checked the others but, they were all cleaned". She paused to take a breath. "I only found that five and a roll of quarters. People prolly looted them during all the chaos". She pouted.

"Let's keep the money,just in case. Wemight need it for trade".

Elise poked Nika in the shoulder, I guess that's one way of disciplining a person. Elise's pokes were not to be messed with. After all that, I still had to decide a winner. They were taking this whole race thing a little too seriously, but I had to satisfy them in some way.I turned my back on the mand paced forward, then hummed, then spun back to face them. They were both eager to hear the results. And I had come up with one.

I clapped my hands two times and made a trumpet noise with my hands.

"You've both shown true talent out there, both contestants proved to be equally strong, but I've made my decision...and the winner to the 300th Walmart biker race is..." I paused, for a more dramatic effect. I swung around and pointed,

"MISS ELISE STANFORD CONGRAGULATIONS"! She screamed and jumped up and down.

"Yus"! She fist pumped the air.

"NO! I gave you money, that's not fair...you're choosing over favorites". Nika stomped her foot, then the other one. I allowed her to do that a couple more times; allowing her to release all the tension before I spoke back, "Nope, it was indeed a close cut, but Elise was ahead by a nose". Elise froze in place, her left hand in a fist, halfway in the air. *Ah, Lord* "What do you mean, she was close by a *nose*"? Nika asked, she huffed.

"A nose, as in; she won..." I really didn't want to finish that sentence. The look on Elise's face was literally a warning. I saw something register in Nikas expression. *I think she got it now.*

"Oh"! She exclaimed, then she turned to Elise and snickered.

"Don't even..." I pointed a finger at her.

"its cause her nose is so big, that's how she won right"? I rubbed my face with a hand, covering my oncoming laugh, in ching a finger so I can peek at Elise. I was surprised to find her to tally calm. I guess that's to be expected, she knew I wasn't making fun of her. But still, I knew that the whole nose thing was a sensitive subject for her. The thing about Elise is that she has a bit of a complex about it. I keep telling her not to mind it, "Don't let it bother you", I remember continuously telling her that. Heck, I think my nose is pretty freaking weird too. *It ain't as big though, but I won't mention that* She breathed in and out, and settled herself down.

"Jade, did you finish making those Molotov's I told you about"? Her voice was strained. She was ready to explode, all it would need is a trigger. *And that would be Nika* "Yes...we've got 10 I put them along with the rest of the stuff in the truck". She nodded at me. I don't know, it was still a little unsettling, she's too calm...*way*too calm. Her eyes were wide and bright, the brightest I've ever seen them, then she began to smile and it was towards me. I would have found it cute in a different situation but right now, it's just freakin me the heck out.

"Thank you, I'm sure that took a long time to do". Her voice settled to a low tempo, I could almost hear the vibrato in her words.

"Yeah well, they could be put to good use, when we need'em". I scratched the back of my head, the air around use was starting to feel

82

uncomfortable. I knew Elise when she gets pissed, and this was way, way beyond that point. *I'm gonna evacuate before the bomb detonates* "Youguys have your walkie' sonya"? I asked them both, they nodded. "I'm gonna head over to the front, check the barricades, keep your walkie's to station 7,I'll report anything Ifind...suspicious".

They both nodded again, I kept my mouth shut and walked towards the front. The store settled around me, a quiet that both relaxed and disturbed me. Nothing but the light squeaking of my boots against the floor, to help put me at ease. I tightened the straps of my katana holder, the clip nearly pinching my skin. I stood infront of the sliding door, to us ling my looses trands of hair before curling it back behind my ears.

"I need a blasted shower". *And a new tank too.* It took me a good three hours to pick out a new tank top. The one I wore was covered in blood, it dried to an unearthly deep brown color. It made my inside scring eat the very sight. I picked off a white cotton spaghetti strapped tank ands tripped out of the old one. It smelled of synthetic downy wash. And that "New shirt" smell. Taking no mind in the fact that the fabric was a little too sheer, that my black bra was totallyviewable. Aside from that it was flexible andt hick.

"It'll do". I untied my hair and slowly combed through the knotted strands, making sure to double tie it back in place.

I looked down, and wondered if I should change my shorts as well. They weren't as blood splattered as my shirt, but I spotted a few holes in the cloth, they should be fine...for a while. But just as a precaution I grabbed a clean pair of jean shorts and tossed it over my shoulder. Then I eyed a dark blue and white ombre' button collar shirt. It was crinkled and in need of an iron. My fingers itched to fold the discarded clothing piled on a display counter. Some habits are hard to break.

I walked back to the sliding doors and jumped. Blood, there was fresh blood on the glass. I noticed it was on the other side, I ignored that small detail, the blood appeared to be smeared across the glass, ending on the far side of the doors, and you could almost make out finger prints. What scared me the most was that the tires we so pains takingly rolled one by one were pushed aside. I leaned in closer, and found the bottom of the right sliding door was shattered, leaving a gapping crawl through hole. Blood tracks smeared the floor, leading towards the store's bathrooms. In a moment I was on full alert. I took in my surroundings.

How could we have not heard the glass shatter? I might have happened when we were distracted with that stupid bike race. With Nika screaming like a howler monkey, I almost socked her right then and there. I fumbled for the walkie on my belt. Tuning it to station 7, "Nika, Elise...you hear me"? White noise, then a few seconds later.

"Yeah, what's up"? Elise sounded fine...better than fine, she sounded like her old self.

"Yes Alpha, this is Charlie...what's the situation, over"? And there goes Nika. I chuckled and pressed the speaker button.

"You don't need to say 'over' Nika". I said. White noise.

"It sounds more official that way, over". She chirped. A rustling noise sounded from inside the bathroom. The sound made my right ear tickle.

"What is it"? Elise asked. I sighed and pressed the walkie closer to my lips.

"There's been a...breach in our defenses". Some more shuffling, it seemed to grow louder the longer I stand here.

"Breach? Why what's happened". Elise sounded concerned. I took a deep breath and pressed again, "I noticed one of the tire stacks slanting, I checked; there's a giant arsehole in one of the doors, and I think one of them is inside. I need you both in the front, now"! I flexed my fingers.

"Rodger". Nika said.

"I'm on my way". Elise cut off before I could reply. I slid the walkie back on my belt and stepped slowly towards the bathrooms. My heart thundered against my chest, I pounded my fist at it, thinking that it would somehow calm it down. Someone tapped my shoulder gently, I spun around, a katana halfway out of its sheath.

"It's just us". Elise whispered behind me. She nodded behind her, Nika was inspecting the shattered hole.

"Situation"? I turned my head towards the bathrooms, and Elise nodded with understanding.

"Found blood tracks, it ain't human...too dark, it lead..." I traced the marks ahead of us straight into the woman's bathroom. "Right in there". She nodded again and took out two long kitchen knives. I grinned at the knives sharpness and looked at Elise.

"Germansteal, very light but cuts through almost everything... great choice". She looked down at the twins and looked up, she nudged my shoulder.

"Only you would know". Once she said that, her face automatically turned to stone, straight, very much poker faced. A woman on a mission.

I trailed behind her, as she walked silently on her toes. We crept closer to the bathroom door. The light above us momentarily flickered, giving off an eerievibe. My breathings lowed, with each step, I unsheathed the katana on my left and held it secured to my side. I gripped the red twine that wrapped around the handle, my thumb caressing the tough mahogany leather.

Elise paused, and pointed a thumb at the door. It was slightly ajar. The ground below the door was covered in blood. Darkest blood color I've ever seen, We waited there, waited for something to happen. I don't know what it was we were looking for, I'm not a patient woman, just standing here without doing anything is making me nervous. It then occurred to me that, Elise was probably waiting for my permission to proceed. Oh, was I put in charge without my knowledge again?

"On my go". I breathed in through my nose and out through my mouth, just like my instructor showed me. I saw a lone bead of sweat dribble down Elise's neck line. Nika paced behind me,

I knew that she was getting excited. But it could only be one of them. I sighed,

"Go". We charged in, as quietly as our heavy combat boots could let us, door swung soundlessly on its hinges. I nodded for Nika to bare the door open, incase we need to runout, Elise was positioned to my right her back against the few faucets in the room, a dirt speckled mirror reflecting us, and the thing in the first stall. I swallowed the lump that made its way into my throat. Relax,justbreath.

Elise looked at me for confirmation. I couldn't take my eyes off the only door that separated us from the undead carcass on the other side. I nodded once, and Elise kicked open the door, it slammed inwardly, the sound echoed against the blue tiled walls.

"Holy..." Nika squeaked from the doorway.

I wanted to look away, but my eyes stayed glued to the thing in front of me. She was covered in blood. From head to toe, I could hardly make out the dirty blond streaks that used to be her hair, I mean...all I saw was

86

black blood. In some places it dried and crusted around the tips of her hair and her face. She was crying, but normally tears would be clear liquid right?

Not thick bloody streaks streaming down her reddened cheeks. Her eyes were blood shot, her pupils were dilated so much that you couldn't tell the iris from the pupil. I stared at her, and she stared back. Empty... black eyes She made no move for me other or the others. I just held onto the katana tightly. I wasn't aware that I was trembling as much as she was, when I heard the sword rattle in my hands.

That's when she looked at the sword, her eyes widened in horror. I flinched when she put up her hands, to cover her face, she crouched low on the ground.

"P-p-please...don-don't". It stuttered. And I found it hard to breath, the air suddenly became too heavy for me. She...it spoke.

"What". When I finally found my voice, it didn't really come out as a question.

"D-don't...p-please, help-". She coughed, and just doing that little task made her whole body tremble. Even the wall of the stall against her back shook. Blood splattered in front of her, spraying the wall in front and the floor around her. I instinctively took a step back, while Elise and Nika stood still asstatues.

"He-help". She croaked, her voice barely a whisper. I waitedfor her to talk more but, her attitude changed, she stilled for a moment, and her breathing sped up.

"Are you..." Her head snapped up, and I knew then that...she was gone for good. She stood up, and growled in my direction.

She started out slow, but then lunged from the stall, towards me.

Everything went into motion.

I jumped out of the way before she could claim me. Her body smashed into the mirror, shards fell to the ground and some stuck to her face. My skin shivered from the sight. She lost her footing but regained it back by trying to swipe at my head with her claw like hands. I ducked out of reach. I motioned for Elise to standby.

Just this little one I could handle by myself.

"Get out". I said to her sternly. She complied by nodding jerkily and rushed out the door, with Nika right behind her.

Chapter 11

I was getting another headache.

"Now it's just you and me". It cocked its head to the side, as if trying to understand me. It snarled and lunged for me again, only this time I reacted. I blocked her hands with the dull edge of the sword, I moved out of the way, switching to the sharp edge I hit the top of her head with the butt of the handle. She stumbled forward, landing on her knees. If it was me in that situation, I would have cried out from the pain. Before she could get up again, I whipped the blade across the air, slicing her head right clean off its shoulders. Blood sprayed from the open cavity. Raining down black blood. After the thing stopped bleeding I stood there in silence. The entire room was covered in blood. Yougetthe day off Mr. Janitor

I was the only one not covered in blood, only specks had made its way onto my shirt but that didn't seem like a problem. Good thing I wasn't in clear range or I would have been caked in blood, I'd hate to change clothes again. I wiped the remaining blood using a disposable paper towel off the blade. There was blood on both my hands, I turned around and rinsed them in the sink, rinsing them until the water ran clear. I looked back at the body, she lay in a large puddle of blood. Her head must be...

"Oh, there you are". Her head was in the far corner of the room. Her eyes wide open, and blank. I calmed myself down before walking out the door. Elise and Nika were leaning against the wall.

"All done". My voice was clipped, and husky. No idea why it was husky.

"That fast"? Nika skipped up to me. Orange speckled green eyes staring into mine.

"Yes". I answered her.

"That's wha-". I turned to Elise sharply.

"Don't even start with that gibberish". I pointed a finger at her, jamming the katana back into the sheath.

"Aheesh, okay calm down". She put her hands up as if to surrender.

"Why you so grumpy"? Nika poked my arm, which by theway still stung like heck from the sun.

"I'mnot". Yetagain...whys my voice soblasted husky? "Yes...you so are". She said again.

"Maybe youjust need to eat". Elise said, she kickedoff the wall and walked over to us.

"Maybe..." Or maybe I just witnessed a person change before my very eyes, then had to decapitate the poor girl.

"I'll go get ya some chocolate...I managed to save some". She winked at me and strode off.

Nika was still poking my arm. I don't know why people like doing that to me. They just don't care about how I feel. She stopped and looked over my shoulder,

"Can I see"? She asked.

"See what"? I glanced in the direction she was staring at. I saw the bathroom door and shook my head.

"No". Flat, straight, no-nonsense tone. "No".

"Huh? Why not, it's not like I'll be freaked out by it. I've had my fair share of killings". It still doesn't make it right for you to see, besides I doubt she's ever seen something like that scene in there. Right out of a slasher flick.

"When I mean no...I mean NO". I'll lock the blasted door if I have to.
"Fine"! She shouted in my face and stomped away. I might have to lock
and brace the door later, I know she'll try to sneak by without me
noticing.

We got together duck tape and cardboard to patch the hole in the door.
It'll have to do for now, we've nothing thicker than the cardboard so, in
case things go wrong at least it'll keep them out long enough for us to
escape.

I think we've been staying here for two weeks now, the lights would
blink on and off some days but, Nika's assured us we'd have a week left
of power. We tried the radio stations, looking out for an emergency alerts,
anything information about the military. So far we've had nothing. I
mentioned that maybe, they gave up on us.

A report was made about the rest of the country, having the same
problem as us. With the population higher in some countries, the bite rates
increased. I'd get glances from Nika and Elise when a new alert sounded
from the radio, we slept less every day. I was always telling them that they
should rest, that I'll keep watch.

"You can't keep watch all the time". Elise bellowed from the
men'sbathroom. Wehadto use the alternative since the woman's was
quarantined.

"Yeah, I can't really sleep well at night when I hear you stalking the
place. It's kinda freaky you know"? Nika was cutting up a white t-shirt to
use for make-shift gauzes.

"Well, one: I go by a different sleep pattern, and two: I can stay awake
as long as I need to, so stop arguing about it". I dropped the notepad I was

91

drawing on. This subject keeps getting brought up, eventually they give up and let me guardthem.

In the three weeks we've sheltered here, the power finally turned off. And we've started to ration our food supply.

"You think we should move on, then"? I asked during lunch.

We lit lanterns around the main areas of the store, since the surveillance cameras are down we've tightened our lock downs and changed our shifts. I'd usually, make rounds three times around the store, checking the front and back doors, checking the few medicines we've dug up in the pharmacy. Elise would double take on the food supply, and I've warned her not to sneak snacks between meals. Too many times to count

Nika would always try the radios, the ones that were on batteries. So far, nothing important came up. It's been quiet. And it worries me.

"Yeah, I think we should. We've already stayed here longer than we should have". Elise was chewing on a jerky stick.

"What does the plan say"? Nika was stretching beside me, I could faintly hear the pops and cracks of her stressed out bones.

She's started this exercise up again, saying that she became lazy during our temporary stay.

"Well, we were supposed to go into the city, or down town.

But, I don't think that'd be a good idea. The Bodies numbers might be more than we can handle in those parts". I said. Messaging my knee caps.

"We haven't heard any news about the city, but I'd guess it might be the best place to look for answers or help". Elise said.

"Heck! We might even be able to jackpot an S.W.A.T truck".

Nika jumped up and down. All the excitement was started to affect her. It's a possibility that the S.W.A.T stopped over in the city to evacuate people, any survivors left over from the evacuation; I doubt they'd take the time to rescue. That's the kind of place this world is.

"That's very unlikely". Elise crumpled the jerky bag and tossed it to the side.

"Don't be negative, I'm sure we'd find a few in the city. There are always S.W.A.T teams during apocalyptic situations...and or situations that need their involvement". Nika settled down next to me and leaned her head on my shoulder.

"More than the S.W.A.T, maybe they left some goodies lying around. If we're gonna fight these things, we're gonna need proper equipment". She nudged my shoulder, her hair tickled my skin; it made me flinch but I did my best not to move. What's more deadly than my fists are my brick like shoulder blades? Trust me they ain't as comfortable as they look "Yes, knives aren't gonna last long where we're going. It would be nice to stumble upon a gun case. I'd like a sniper rifle". Elise has this thing about sniper rifles. Ever since her exciting introduction to the first person shooter "Call of Duty" she's been hooked on guns. Now, maybe it might have been a bad idea to allow her access to these kinds of things, but I couldn't help it. I thought that she would like it, I didn't think I'd turn her into a shooting beast. And okay, real life shooting doesn't compare to video games but I know for sure that she'd be perfect for the sniper position. I mean, ever since I took her to that shooting range in CYou know what that's not really important right now.

"I've always wanted twinpistols, like double wielding. That'd be pretty awesome". Her voice was in a whisper, and I felt her head grow heavy on my shoulder. I patted her head and told her to take a nap. She whined at first but, I managed to persuade her. She moved around behind

93

me and plopped down on the make-shift bed, that we made from a king sized comforter and a couple pillows.

I looked back and she was already snoring lightly. Out like a light

"She's sleeping more lately, should I be worried"? I turned back to Elise. She looked behind me at Nika then looked back at me.

"No, she's just exhausted. And she's gonna need all the sleep she can get". I remember Nika used to sleep constantly, even when I would come over their house to hang out she'd be asleep.

And her reasons would be; either she's had a long day,or she isn't feeling well.

"Okay, what about you"? To be honest Elise looked paler than usual, and the bags under her eyes have begun to turn a light shade of purple. I'm not gonna tell her that though, then she'd try to argue about how she doesn't need sleep, that she's perfectly fine and capable of staying alert. I just won't say anything at all

"I'm fine". See?

"Alright". And we ended the conversation there. Afterwards, Elise got up and took her shift to patrol the store, Nika wasstill sleeping, and I sharpened the blades on the katana's. (Fortunate enough to find a lead block for sharpening)

We continued this cycle for a good three days, then finally after our last meeting, we all decided to head for the city. Elise and Nika still wanted to get in touch with their folks, while I worried about mine. I didn't like the topic when it came up but we had to think about worst case scenarios. If we managed to find their folks we could all escape out of state and search for a safe haven. I mentioned that the worst thing that could happen, was if my mom didn't make it. She's a strong woman yes but, this is reality and

I know that it maybe already too late.

Elise and Nika tried to cheer me up, I didn't cry...no I'd never cry in front of them. For now, I need to clear my head and think about what's happening for us.

The next day, we rolled up a few blankets and packed it into the truck. Taking more snacks along for each of us, we hopped into the truck and crossed our fingers. When we had our opening, Elise stomped on the accelerator and the car lurched forward, my head pressed hard against the seat. It felt like my brain shook loose and tossed itself inside my head. I had to roll my window up, zombie brains and white tank top do not mix well you know?

She took a sharp turn left towards the parking lots exit. And I gotta say, she kicks arse. There were so many of those things out here. The tires screeched to a halt, and I looked in there-view mirror.

"Holy heck, I've only ever seen this many bodies in zombie movies". Nika screamed from behind me. She was up on the seat with her back against us, her feet extended out on top of the arm rest between me and Elise. Excited aren't we?

I turned to Elise, she gave me one of those looks. I didn't like where this was going, I shook my head and she gestured to the back. I looked again at the re-view mirror and a couple of Bodies limped towards the truck. They were perfectly positioned near the rear bumper. I heard Elise slap her hands together and jerked the truck into reverse. I braced my hands in front of me before my body slammed into the dashboard. I felt my left pinky bend unnaturally, and the pain shot up my wrist. I squeezed my eyes shut telling myself to relax, that the pain will go away.

The truck hopped up and down, and shook all around us.

"What the heck Elise"! Nika screeched, I found her on the floor her neck was at an odd angle, her left leg on the seat and her right kicked upwards. I turned to Elise and gave her the stank eye.

She peeked from under her lashed and gave a slight nod, putting the truck back in drive. It sprung up one last time making my head bump against the window, and it continued its course on the deserted street. When things calmed down, I took a look at my pinky and winced. It looked even worse than it felt. The tip bent backwards, I swear if I could it would have touch the knuckle. The nail was split and blood leaked from the brokenskin.

"Ugh, oh god...that is...that's just-". I felt Nika examining my pinky, just like me; couldn't finish her sentence. The whole thing left me speechless.

"Is it broken"? Elise asked her eyes never leaving the road.

"Well, No Elise it's not broken...it just likes to bend that way sometimes for good fun"! My voiced cracked. She smirked at me and told Nika to fetch the first-aid kit.

"You don't have to be an arse about it". She said.

"I can if I wanna be an arse about it, know why? Because of your little stunt my pinky is now bent beyond recognition, the bone would have torn through the skin! I'd look just like those things".I pointed at the bloodied car casses that roamed the streets around us. They looked even worse than before, the morning sun rose high in the sky, and baked the ground. For a minute I swore I could have sniffed barbecued rotted skin.

"You can just line the bone back in place and wrap it, you'll be fine". She sighed. I eyed her again and snarled. She shot me a confused glance.

"Want me to break all of your fingers? And I'll tell ya to just wrap em' and ignore the freakin pain...don't test me Elise". I cracked my knuckles (the available ones) and started for her hand. She flinched.

"God, Jade I'm driving"! She huffed. "I'm sorry alright"?! I clicked my tongue and plopped back down on my seat.

"Here". Nika gave me the first-aid kit. Elise glanced at me a couple times as I tried to put the bone back. I've never done this before, and I've only seen it on T.V.

It took me a couple tries to put it back, the first; and I couldn't even think it was possible...to bend it even more than it already is. And the second, I chickened out because of the pain. Then finally,

I bit down on a folded cloth and jerked the boneforward.

"Geez..." Nika winced behind me. I groaned and took the medical tape, wrapping it around the now bruising pinky.

"You gonna be okay? I mean, you able to use the katana with... um". Well, Elise stuttering. This is very shocking.

"It's not impossible, but I'm sure I'll be able to manage using only four fingers".

"You're very first broken bone"! Nika chirped.

"Yeah, way to start the day off with a broken pinky".

Chapter 12

It took about a half an hour to get down town. There wasn't much to hear on the radio; more news feed about the epidemic.

The military seems to be doing a fine job of holding back those things. And so far, no safe havens have popped up. Weknew that it would only take a matter of months for them to actually pull it off. Meanwhile, the human race is going extinct.

We passed by a couple of shops, and restaurants that looked like they were still doingbusiness, aside from the constant bodies roaming head of the shops and sidewalks, the town looked decent.

I'm not sure what I really expected from this part of the town, for some reason it looked like the apocalypse hadn't even happened at all.

"Kinda reminds me of a movie set". I said to myself. Elise chuckled beside me and swerved the truck, turning a left corner.

"The heck..." My blood ran cold and the shivers racked my body so heavily that I felt I was going to vomit right there.

"Well, now we know where all the people went". Nika mumbled from the back seat. The scene was too much for me to bare.

I wanted to turn away from it all but, for some reason my eyes stayed glued to it. The space inside the truck fell silent; as we viewed up on the thousands of bodies lying on the heated cement.

They laid unmoving and there was just so much blood that even I couldn't handle it. Elise took a sharp intake of breath and pressed on through the sea of still Bodies. I counted at least hundreds of them scattered here and there. Some stacked up in a pile and I wondered who had the time to do all of that. *Who could do all of this?*

"It's creepy how you know their all dead...and the fact that they won't move at all". Nika was oddly quiet when she said this, my ears strained on her voice.

"You think the military swept through here for Evac"? Elise gripped the steering wheel until the whites of her knuckles showed, it was strange against her already pale skin.

"I guess, I noticed some recent tire marks going off into the East". She pointed towards a cleared path a couple blocks away from us. We kept heading straight. I tried to ignore the piles of flesh stacked into neat piles along the sidewalks. So many have died in a matter of weeks, it was unbelievable. I looked at the gas meter for a distraction and noticed that it was nearly gone.

"We need to refill the tank". I mentioned to Elise who was, astonishingly very calm at the moment. *How utterly disturbing Stanford* "It'll run for a few more hours, we'll find a gas station and try to get some gas. If not, well siphon gas from other cars". I looked at her oddly.

"You know how to siphon gas from other cars"? I asked. She turned her head and gave me an impish grin; that occurred so rare that I scolded myself for not taking a picture of it.

"Indeed I do". She said matter of factly.

"I do too"! Nika shouted. As did I...and of course this comes from watching movies that involves such an act, and some info from websites on "How to's". Oh mother would be so proud to know that her little girl knows how to steal gas from other cars. *Among other things...* We took a moment of stillness, all but our heavy breathing emitted from the silence. We took another left around the corner, and stopped at a small stripmall.

Multiple shops lined the oval shaped space. Lots of cake shopsand restaurants. I've come here a couple of times in the past, I'd like to call this the sweets and salts circle, again the place is shaped like an oval. *No idea why I called it a circle.* I'm guessing my little 8 year old mind wasn't able to process things as clearly as I could now. *Heck, it still takes a century for me to figure out something* Elise eased into a small parking lot. Lone cars sat idly, scattered on the pavement. They appeared to be in good use, nothing but some of the windows smashed in, some flat tires.

"Let's see if we can scavenge some things here". Elise said, she placed the truck in park and popped the door open. Both me and Nika got out, and eased the doors shut quietly. Just because there weren't any Bodies nearby, doesn't mean they couldn't hear us slamming the doors.

"So, where would you like to start first?" Elise looked to us. I noticed that she was decked out in weaponry. If you could count a hand full of kitchen knives, two steal baseball bats, and an iron hammer acceptable weapons. *I'd say I do, think they are...quite menacing actually.*

I noticed a lone knife handle sticking out of her boots. As long as you don't accidentally cut yourself with that sucker... "The cake shop obviously". Nika drawls. I look at her and then at Elise. She gives me a pointed look, *I'm guessing you'd like to check out the cake shop out too?*

"Sure why not?" I say finally. I can already heart he squeals from both of them. They needn't express that openly, I'd fear for the worst. I highly doubt that there would be anything useful there, and I highly doubt there would be any sweets left. I mean c'mon, in any situation like this who wouldn't grab all the sweets and run like heck away. I sighed, and followed the two idiots inside the store.

The door was left slightly ajar, I thought oddly about it, then looked up. *Ah, that might have made some noise.* Two silver bells hang loosely above the doorway. Elise must have noticed too before entering. A rolled up magazine is wedged into the corner of the door, allowing it to close softly and partly.

As I suspected, nothing remains in the glass cases. Shards of glass scatter the flooring, nothing but the crunching of my boots upon them in the tiny shop. Nika and Elise are nowhere in sight, until I hear a bit of noise coming from the back. Shuffling, then muffled giggles. I try not to roll my eyes when I enter the kitchen.

Layers of flour cover the floor, cart sand baking utensil saree very where. I found the two drawing on the metal table in the center of the room. Doodles here and there in the flour. "High life" is scrawled in cursive on one corner. *Really Nika?*

I walk over to them, Elise is crouching, her hands wandering inside a large pantry. Nika is to the side nibbling on something that might have been drenched in chocolate. I elbow Nika,

"What's that ya got there?" I ask. Notingher chocolate covered hands and mouth. The scene looks somewhat unsettling. *If that were blood, I think I'd vomit* "Elise found some chocolate dipped donuts". She said, I can already see the sugar taking effect in her too bright eyes.

"When you mean *some...*" I looked around.

"I ate them all". She shrugged sticking her tongue out slightly.

"Didn't think to share thetreasure, huh?" I could bemad, yeah I could be. But I choose not to be. Why? Well, I'm assuming that if I'd gotten here sooner I'd be walking myself into a war zone.

I could survive without chocolate for a while. As for the two idiots... give or take 10 hours. Although, I do need some sustenance every few days, I could go into withdrawal. Seriously. Health wise, I have to eat some sort of food that will keep my body from collapsing in on itself. It's a scary thing.

"Nah, once I pulled them out of the pantry she swiped the donuts away from me. She was like, deadly fast". Elise straightened up onto her feet, holding large white boxes in her arms. I eased a few from her and placed them on the counter top. I think I hit my head a while back because the scene in front of me might as well have been due to a concussion. A full spread of all kinds of pastries line the counter. It's like a freakin gold mine!

"W-what..." Whoever came here before us to scavenge, they sure didn't look hard enough.

"What a spread!" *Took the words right out of my mouth Nika.*

"Don't eat all of it! Take a few, then save the rest for later".

Elise gave a pointed look to Nika. Nika peeked over the pile of sweets in her arms and scowled.

"I should be the one yelling at you. Planning on eating all of those?" I turned my head back to Elise, she was stuffing packages of muffins and cookies in a black duffel bag.

"This a robbery or something? What's with the black duffel?" I leaned a hip against the counter.

"Was' the biggest bag I could find when we were at

Walmart". *Yeah, but a black duffel?*

"All that food's gonna spoil ya'know?" I picked up alone raisin oatmeal cookie and examined it. *So much raisin...*

"Not, if we preserve it the correct way". She huffed, zipping the bag shut and balanced it over her shoulder.

"Preserve as in...You'll eat everything in a matter of minutes".

I took a bite from the oatmeal cookie, and made a face at the consistency. I gagged and spit the chewed up crap into the garbage.

"I thought you liked that kind". Nika was perched atop the counter opposite me, nibbling on a muffin from her stash.

"Yeah, these people obviously have no idea how to make it the right way. The heck was with the flavor?" I threw the rest of the cookie into a corner. "It was crunchy, the thing irritated the heck out of my teeth". *Like freakin sand paper.*

"Not everyone is as good a baker as you, Jade". Elise tossed a few chocolate covered almonds in her mouth. She spoke, "Times are touf mow, woo can't be picky wif food anymore".

I glared at her, "What did I say about talking with your mouth full?" She stopped and stared at me for a few seconds. Then began chewing again.

"Sorry, *mom*". She flung an almond at me, I managed to dodge in time before it was able to hit my eye. I frowned. She smirked and walked back into the hallway.

"And no mocking!" I shouted back. Geez, was that too loud? I turned back to Nika, who by the looks of things was finishing her pile of sweets.

"You done in here, or are you still searching?" I asked her. She shook her head slightly and hopped off the counter. She jogged into the hallway leaving a trail of crumbs on thefloor. I paced the kitchen, looking into the other pantries they haven't looted yet. Nothing of use, a few boxes of sweets mostly decorations and fondant. I walked into the very back of the shop and checked the office. It was compact yet comfortable. A thin black Mac desktop filled the space of a small mahogany desk. Sheets of paper

104

litter the floor, some information left pinned to the walls. A couple of pictures scattered here and there, of perhaps the people that ran the shop. I only glanced at their faces, no use trying to remember how they looked. *They may be dead.*

I shook my head in frustration and exited the room. I checked the back entrance and found it locked. Nothing has been disturbed. Walking back towards the front I heard the shuffling of feet, maybe a few feet away from where I stood. They were heavy and weary. Not at all like Elise's has who stridden with purpose or Nika's light foot falls. My heart began to hammer against my chest.

It couldn't be one of those things either. I took a couple breaths in and exhaled through my nose. Silent.

I took my time, my fingers skimming the wall beside me. The shuffling stopped. I stood there for a good while, listening to the sounds echoing against the cream plaster walls. The air was stifling, it got hotter and it irked me somehow for not noticing until now.

A scrap sounded ahead of me, I eased one foot in front of the other, careful not to make a sound of my own. *The element of surprise.*

I reached slowly behind my back for the katana. The black leather hilt held firm in my grasp. Once I got to the corner of the hall, I crouched down low and waited. An eerie silence stretched across the space. My still panting breathe the only sound.

Scratching, shuffling

Quiet voices filled the silence. Their murmurings too soft to make out. *But their definitely human.* Doesn't mean they ain't dangerous. I nodded to myself and bent my knees. In a midcrouch I drifted towards the voices. "- were here. The place is cleared out already". A small voice rang out.

"Let's check the back then". Another, deep and sure.

"What about the Hummer in front?" This person sounds tired, his voice is scratchy. Is he sick?

"If you're so hyped on the Hummer then get you're scrawny arse to it, we ain't the only ones lookin' for a ride". He sounds... well, pissed. And the kind of guy I'll most likely hate upon meeting. I groaned inwardly, just what I need...inconveniences. I sighed, and loosened my grip on the handle. *They seem like trouble, especially the men, but maybe...If I played it out right-* "Who the heck are you mongrels!?" Nikas high pitched voice boomed into the shop. *Oh great. Just great!*

She could have let me handle this my way. I stood up and walked into what I would call, *a freakin mess of all messes.* Four people stood in a circle in the center of the shop. They all had make-shift weapons in their hands, their clothes dirty, dried blood splattered against them from their killings. They stood in formation,theirbodiesturnedtowardsNika. Shealreadyhadher own weapons on display. Two knitting picks in each hand and a somewhat threatening glare in her eyes. *This is not good. Do something you nitwit!*

I relaxed my body, and leaned against the glass case. The sheath of my katana knocking lightly against it. The four jumped and turned towards me. This way I could get a better view of who I might have to go against. There were three men and a women. She might be a little older than me, but it's hard to tell with all the dirt on her face. *Wow, they look so worn. I wonder how I must look to them.*

The smallest of the three men, was indeed *scrawny.* I was almost concerned for him. His limbs were willowy, his complexionpasty. Sweat dribbled down his hallow face and lazy brown eyes peeked from long frayed black bangs. *He does look sick...did they notice?* Maybe I'm being paranoid.

I looked to the right of him, and there stood a heavy set man.

Late thirties I would assume. That with the thick beard on his face, tiny gray hairs were visible. And might I add, he was bald.

Does he like polish that thing? Lord! It's totally winking against the sunlight.

I mentally slapped myself not to stare for too long at it. And that I didn't need to thanks to his beady black eyes literally staring holes into me. I crossed my arms against my chest and gave them all a steady look. *Alright you can do this.*

Chapter 13

Good afternoon". I nodded to each of them. They looked at each other and back to me puzzled. "Be at ease, we don't want any trouble. We're just a couple of gals looking for some food, no harm done there. We're already done searching, so we'll be on our way.Hm?" I gave them my best comforting smile. *Which works wonders* They all eased a fraction, weapons still in hand. I sighed and motioned to Nika.

"Put those things away, there's no need for them". With that, I gave her a look. The look which says, *'I'm not messing around, I'm totally serious, so you better listen to me or I'll do something to right you'*. She physically shook and placed her weapons back into her belt strap.

"We're all just trying to survive here, surely you must understand the precautions". I swear it took them at least an eternity to nod in agreement and tuck awaytheir own weapons. *Thank...you* I glanced to the wall, and found the final member of their little group. As he leaned casually against the wall, he stared right at me. His arms crossed over a... let's see, wide chest. I took my time looking over this mysterious being. He's older, maybe by a few years. I started at his shoes, black track boots perfect for running and hiking laced tightly around well-muscled calves. Like all the others his clothes were dirty with dried blood and dirt. What...

tracked upwards, loose fitting dark jeanshung...perfectly around narrow hips. *Oh...* Before I knew what I was doing, my eyes roamed over what his sweat soaked short sleeve shirt could provide, defined abs peeked through the thin cotton. Toned arms flexed once, twice. *My...* Finally, my eyes made it upto his face. God! Astrong square jaw jutted out of a tanned face.

His nose pointed and even. *Not like that crow like muzzle the pasty dudes sporting.*

Thank goodness I had something to lean against for support because I would have ended up sprawled on the floor unconscious. Surrounded by full lashes, his eyes—good lord his eyes.A light shade of storm gray. I've no way else to describe the color.

Clearly I lack in vocabulary skills...again. What have I just walked into? And how the heck has this Greek god not shown himself to me until now? *Is this fate playing with my life again? Because this ain't fair! I wasn't prepared!*

"Do you use the same old line every time you come across someone?" He spoke. Jeez, even his voice sounds sexy. Keep it together!

I switched positions and settled my weight on the other leg.

"No, I just want to assureyouguys, that my peoplearen't trouble, that I'm not trouble. Unless, you give me a reason to be".

There!

He nodded slightly. And smirked. *Holy mother Mary, why have I not noticed those lips sooner?* I've only ever seen lips like those in magazines. He's gotta be a model or something, I mean c'mon.

Okay, enough gawking, focus. I noticed Nika still standing in the doorway of the shop, her gaze locked on Mr. Man.

I cleared my throat, and Nika snapped her head back to me.

"Where's you're sister?" I asked. Making sure not to look at...him.

She shrugged, "Dunno, She told me to wait in the truck while she looks at the store next door-".

"She did what?!" I really hope my eyes weren't about to pop out of their sockets.

She shrugged again this time with a jerk. "Ah, she also told me not to tell you. Said you'd overreact about her safety and what not".Here yes were roaming around the room, looking anywhere but where I stood. How can she be so stupid? Sure the store over was pretty close but what if...

"Did you see any Bodies outside?" I started forward not even paying attention when the three losers stepped back with their weapons drawn again.

"A couple, but they were far off—jade I think you should calm down..." She placed both her hands in front to, protect herself?

Maybe? Just how pissed did I look?

"I'll calm down when I wring you're sisters neck". Course I won't do it.

I was half way towards the outside when a firm hand gripped my arm. I shivered at the sudden contact and spun around. I had to crane my head back farther than what I was used to took look at the giant in front of me. I'm like, five-six but this dudes probably six feet and infinity! *Okay, so maybe I might've exaggerated, like six-three or so.*

Long fingers tightened around my arm, and I winced. Hopefully not outwardly. "W-what?" Oh yes, the stuttering has begun!

"Where exactly do you think you're going?" He stared down at me. Is he glaring? And do I detect a bit of teasing in those eyes?

"I-I'm gonna g-go look for my f-friend". *Don't stutter you fool!* A corner of those tempting lips perked up slightly. Oh god—is he getting closer?

"It's rude to leave in the middle of a conversation. Even ruder to leave without telling me your name". He spoke slowly as if I were child, as If I were slow in the head. Maybe I am slow in the head. I can't even process anything at the moment. Nika help me! "J-Jade...it's Jade". I answered in a whisper.

"Jade". He repeated back. He even makes my name sound dirty when he says it.Alright, it's enough right? Let go of my arm before you rip it off!

"Uh..." I tried to tug my arm away but, it was like it was encased in steal.

"Good to meet ya' I'm Evan". He jabbed his thumb towards the three behind him. "Big guy is Tony, skinny fellow is Dean, and the lady is Samantha or Sam". He didn't even look at them during the introduction. *Someone shoot me...soon.*

"Uh-huh". I can't even talk anymore. I'm done. At that his smirk turned into a full on grin. *I'm dead...yep.*

"Wasn't so bad huh? Didn't take too much of your time right?" he wasjust too close to me. And the fact that his voice got husky— which doesn't help my current situation the least bit. *Anyone...*

"Am I interrupting something?" The lust filled smog cleared right outofmy head,Ijerked my arm free andwhippedmy attentionto my one and only savior.

"Nope, not at all. In fact you saved me from making the worst decision of my life". I shot a dirty look towards Evan and hid behind Elise. Placing both hands on her shoulders, I heaved a heavy sigh.

"Thank god, you've returned. I was gonna kill you for leaving Nika behind to check the other store, you could've waited". Ah! Today is just so exasperating.

"I've no patience when it comes to that girl. It was an in—out operation, barely took me ten minutes to search the place". She looked back at me and to Evan. "Who's this person?" I snook a peek over her shoulder, he was still grinning like the arsehole I've now tagged him to be, he caught my look and raised an eyebrow. *Could Elise feel my hands warming?*

"That's Evan, the three over there are Tony, Dean and Samantha". Hopefully she'll rule out who's who, I'm too tired to explain it myself.

"Okay...and when did you all get here?" Her tone no-nonsense like. She was poised, a hand on her hip, back straight, chin up. *Are ya gonna rumble Elise?*

"I'd say, half an hour or so ago. You must be the one Jades been screamin' about". Evan has this weirdly alluring air about him. And tell me I'm not being egoistical or something but, he's been looking at me the entire time...right? I mean I'm not all that interesting to look at. Personally if I were a guy I'd probably look once then stalk off without a second glance, that or otherwise.

"You? My names Elise by the way, thank you for asking. And the one with the goo-goo eyes is my little sister Nika". I suppressed a chuckle.

"Goo-I don't have goo-goo eyes!" She shrieked, shaking her head from side to side. In rapid motion, she stilled and I might have been surprised but I knew the peaceful moment wouldn't last forever. I righted myself and turned towards the door. Nika was inside the shop in seconds, she darted to our side producing her deadly knitting picks in each hand. I had my hold on the hilt of the katana, ready tocharge at any given moment. Elise wasby my side baseball bat held firm against her hip.

We turned towards the door and heck, what do you know. *A couple* turned into about thirty of those things. *It's a horde.*

I looked behind me and found Evans grin gone, in its place something else. Hate? Determination? A sort of fire in his eyes, told me that the playful Evan has disappeared for the moment. *Still, that face is even hotter than that cocky grin he had on earlier.* I shook out my arms, loosening the muscles from when they tensed in his presence. The decaying monsters came closer to the shop, looking even worse here than they were where we came from. *Game face on, game face.*

Shouldn't be a problem, thirty against seven. Hopefully those behind me knew how to fight their way out of this. I can take on three at a time. Just need to pull through smoothly.

"Okay, let's go-". A fit of coughing sounded from behind. I turned towards the noise and gasped. I knew it. Dean had his arms braced against the glasscase. His backbones peaked against his long sleeve shirt. *I hope no one's squeamish in this room.* His breathing labored, he gagged and hacked, black liquid shooting out of his mouth onto the glass. After a few moments of watching him shower the case in blood, he stilled, a low growl emitted from him. His skin took on a more ashen color. His body swayed, I clutched the handle producing a sound from the leather. He turned to the noise; glazed over gray eyes met mine, dark drool dripping down his chin to the floor from his nose and mouth. This is wrong, so fudging wrong.

Chapter 14

Inever knew my thought process was so excessively slow. Or maybe the scene happening in front of me, was just slowing down fraction by fraction.

"Hold him back!" Evan shouted towards Tony. Everything became a blur in a matter of seconds. Tony tried to hold back Dean, but totally underestimated his strength. Dean latched onto Tony's arm, he struggled to break free, and he didn't notice the puddle of blood on the floor and slipped right into Dean's arms. Dean how led be foresinking his teeth intoTony's arm. His screams practically shattering my ear drums.

"Tony!" I didn't even notice Samantha's small form huddled in the corner of the room. She tried to race towards him, but I caught her hand and yanked her to my side. For someone so small she was stubborn, her sobs so loud even that rose above the incoming threats outside the shop. She wriggled in my arms, fighting my hold.

"Hey!" Her head snapped towards my voice, she stared at me, tears streaking down her dirt covered face.

"H-help him!" She bawled.

"I can't! He's gone". I wish I could have been a little more sensitive but all the sensitivity in me flew out the window. She has to learn to get over the loss right now and fast. Still she kept crying, her fingers dug into my arm. The sting from her nails did nothing to me.

"Jade!" I looked to the door, Elise was outside next to the Hummer. They were everywhere. Elise and Nika held them off brilliantly, steal batflying through the air smashing heads. Nika's knitting picks jutting out

115

of eyeballs here and there. *Girls got great aim.*

When one of them got too close, Elise ran up close behind it, kicking its legs out from below. Its head banged loudly against the shop window. When it tried to get up, Elise finished it off by slamming the steal bat into the thing shead. Black blood exploded from the impacts pattering the thick glass window. She must have slammed her all into that one hit, because the sorry suckers head gave through, forever mid-stuck in between theglass.

"The heck are ya' waitin' for? Get in the blasted truck!" Elise sprinted towards the driver's side and yelled at Nika to get in. I looked at Samantha who shook violently, her knuckles white from gripping my arms. I blinked, Evan was already shoving me out the door.

"C'mon".

Minutes passed, then hours. The blazing morning days unturned into a cooling night. Nika's still form breathing silently in the back seat. Her head lolling from side to side.

"She's dead to the world now". Elise spoke. Her eyes weary yet trained ahead.

"Yeah, it's been a long day". I lifted my hand to inspect the healing pinky. The bandage red around the nail.

"What happened there?" Evans voice, was a nodd change in the trucks atmosphere, he was so quiet I hardly knew he was there.

"Oh, I uh...I broke it". *Because Elise decided to be a hot shot.*

"How did you break you're *pinky* finger of all things?" I leaned back in my seat, and instantly regretted it. I felt his hot breath at the base of my neck. *Why did I have to go and sweep my hair to the side? And why is he so blasted close I could feel his freakin breath?!*

116

"Well, it was due to...*someone's* idiotic thinking. It wasn't so bad, it only hurts a little now".

"Who's this someone of whom you speak of?" his voice a low timbre against my ear. *Okay, now I'm getting suspicious. Dude quit now or you'll find your own black boot shoved up you're-*

"I said I was sorry. You're never gonna let it go, huh?" Elise glanced my way, a small enough smirk working its way up her lips unnoticed unless you were really looking.

"Sorry' ain't gonna cut it, no matter how many times you say it.

It was a stupid idea and now you have to bare the consequences of said action". She sighed and drummed the steering wheel with her fingertips.

As I eased my hand back down, Evan gently took hold of it, pulling my hand closer to his face.

"Isn't it about time you...redress this wound, the blood will seep through and the scent might attract unwanted attention".

I sucked in a breath, and exhaled shakily. Don't touch me right now...I swear- I nod instead, not trusting my voice. He asks Elise for the first-aid kit, she looks at him through the rear view mirror and tells him it's underneath the seat. Still holding onto my hand he bends over and sit's back up with the case in his other hand.

It's a bit uncomfortable to sit straight ahead, so I turn my body sideways, and lean against the armrest.

He opens the case and takes out a roll of bandage wrap and antiseptic wipe. I didn't realize I was goggling at him until Elise poked my cheek. I blinked on ceand turned my head slowly in her direction. She gave me one of her signature smirks that says, *you can't hide it Jade, it's showing all over your face. I reply with my own little smirk, Nothings showing. And yes he is one fine specimen of a man but I can't.*

She frowns in response and shakes her head. *I guess that's the end of that, great chat.*

"How does this not hurt like heck?" I swing back my attention to the man behind me. He is staring at my pinky in worry. *Worry?*

Bro, you just met me and you're worried?

"Like I said, it doesn't hurt anymore". He looks at me and it takes all of my will power not to turn into mush from his stormy gaze. In all my 17 years, I never thought I'd meet a guy; well, technically he's not the first I've noticed. I've been in a couple of relationships in the past but they've never been...what's the term—real? I mean, it always starts with the friendship stage, then moves on to the development of romantic feelings stage, then at the end we get together just because we've become interested in one another. They don't always last long. Sure, we had fun and did all those cliché couple stuff, but in the end we're both looking the other way, finding new people. So, relationships don't work for me; and I'm sure they never will. Still, it doesn't mean I can't browse around candy store now does it?

"Besides the bleeding it looks okay, no signs of infection and the bone's in place". Carefully, He starts to wrap a clean bandage around my pinky. He reaches into the case and takes out a small roll of medical tape, taking a small portion of it and sticking it to the loose cloth, he tucks the rest away and sighs. *Are you done now?*

"Okay, good as new". When he let's go of my hand, I immediately miss the warmth. *Stop it Jade, don't do this to yourself. You need to focus on what's important right now.*

I have no idea why I feel this way, maybe because I'm usually always nervous around good looking guys? Nah, can't be.

"Thanks". I mumble. He smiles and leans back to put the case away. I turn back around in my seat and face forward. It's been what? Half a month since shiznit hit the fan, and all the stress is starting to catch up to me. *Margaritas by the seaside sounds great right about now.* Of course, I don't plan on drinking by the way that would be dangerous and foolish. I wouldn't be able to think straight buzzed. Liquor and sharp objects don't mix ya' know? Bit."

Chapter 15

Take a right here". *Ooh, am I dreaming? I've never dreamed about hot guys before and surely not one who's voice makes my body tremble.*

"Upahead, that red building—okay,parkhere".Thetruckrolls to a stop, my body still free floating at the edge of unconsciousness. I feel a warm hand against my skin.

"Hey, Jade. Wake up". *Five more minutes. In fact, let me sleep forever.* "Is she dead?" I hear Nika's voice in the background, but everything else sounds muffled. *I'm so blasted tired.* Then a light slap, as if someone hit something.

"You don't gotta be violent, I'm just asking cause she looks so still!" My ears flinch from the loud noise. I want to wake up.

Apparently both my eyes think otherwise. The truck shakes along with the sound of someone shifting. The warm hand leaves my arm, and I am too tired to snatch it back. Then I feel it against my forehead, letting out a soft sigh.

"She's a little warm..." The voice is soothing. *Don't take away your hand! It feels good on my skin.*

"A little? What do you mean by a little?" Elise is next to me, concern in her voice. I feel another hand reach me and caress my cheek. *Mm, god I hope I never wake up.*

"I mean, it's nothing to worry too much over. She's just worn out, and from the looks at the sunken purple bags under her eyes, it may be due from over working". Both hands are smoothing over my hair and down to my neck. *Not my neck!*

"I told her to rest so many times before. But, she'd wave me off and give some stupid excuse about how she's 'nocturnal' or 'doesn't need a silly thing called sleep'". Anger and worry are warring against each other. I think she wants to be mad at me but, she can't help but agonize over me. A deep chuckle tremors the air.

"She just wants to prove to you guys how strong willed she is. I could tell that you're both very important people to her, and maybe stressing over you're guys' safety is important to her".

The hands stop roaming over my face and disappear. *No! Come back!*

"Yeah? Or maybe she's just being hardheaded". *Ouch.* Well, hardheadedness runs in the family so she's right about that.

Enough of this. I start to open my eye lids slowly, and flinch at the bright light in my face. I groan loudly and cover my eyes with my hands. *I'm blind!*

"Easy...be careful opening your eyes, the suns directly in front of you". *Yes sir!* When the sting subsides, I block the suns glare with my hand and peel one eye open. Then the next open. I have to blink a couple of times for the bright lights to stop dancing at the corners of my vision. *This sucks.*

"Good morning, sunshine". Bright green eyes stare back at me. Elise has here lbows leaning against the middle arm rest, more stray hairs have escaped her pony tail, and the strands stick to her face like glue. *I should tell her to fix that.*

"Don't start". I snap. I have a right to be grumpy, I'm beat and I'm debating whether or not I should go back to sleep or get off my lazy arse. "What time is it?"

"It's ten past nine in the morning". I look to my left and Evan is even closer than I would like him to be. I noticed a few things I couldn't have last night in the dark lighting. His dark brown hair frames his face in loose waves, the ends reaching the back of his shirt collar. The humidity making the tips curl having him combing back the waves with his hand every couple a minutes.

He's also a lot younger than I thought him to be. Interesting.

"Oh, that explains why the sun sabusing me right now". I must have slept in a bad position because now, there's a painful crick in my neck.

I sit up and stretch my arms up, rolling my head from side to side.

"The sun is abusing you?" Evan questions with amusement. I yawn twice and rub my eyes.

"Yes. The sun likes to abuse me with its blasted brightness. I can already feel my energy draining out of me". I lift my hand and look out the window. And it's not just me the suns tormenting today, the black cement looks to be boiling, tar is oozing from the cracks. As if one step outside would put you ablaze. *I may not be a vampire but this would torch the heck out of my skin.*

"Oh, don't be so dramatic. It's not as hot out there as it looks".

I glare up at Elise and scoff.

"Well, not everyone is so gung-ho about the heat as you are".

She squints back at me and laughs.

"Interesting choice of words Jade. "Gung-ho", and where on Earth did you learn that from?" She sit's up and crosses her arms.

"Obviously from movies—and don't youdare go on about my word choice, I've already got the undead on my arse and I don't need a blasted grammar Nazi chasing after". *I really don't need this at nine in the morning.*

"I wasn't going to. And no, I'm not on friendly terms with the heat either, but maybe I'm not as sensitive as you are". She snickers and turns to the front.

"That...was entertaining!" Nika is laughing behind us, her face scrunched up from the act.

"Are they always like this?" Evan asks Nika. I'm trying to ignore his presence. I'm practically fighting with my inner *demon.*

Demons. Their too persistent.

"Every blasted day! It's even better than T.V, I can give you that". She's holding her stomach, bending over the seat. Her laughs muffled.

"Anyways...where are we?" I scanned the barren parking lot. Save for a few cars in the distance.

"Uh, we are at a survivor's refuge...apparently". Elise gripped thewheel. A survivor's refuge? Since when has there been one and why haven't we heard it on the radio?

"Really?"

"Yeah, while you were asleep Evan told us about this refuge that he and a couple other people created a little ways out of town.

At first I wasn't sure if I should trust him, but both him and Sam assured me that he wasn't tricking us". She cleared her throat. I turned back to Evan, I didn't realize he moved even closer when the tips of our noses brushed against each other. I flinched back, bumping into the dashboard with my elbow.

"Careful...wouldn't want you to break another finger". He chuckled. "Oh yeah, we definitely wouldn't want that. Also, there's this little thing called 'personal space' you might've heard of it?" A grin broke out on his face, and I suppressed the urge to punch it right off.

"Take it easy Jade". Nika chirped. She laid her head against the

124

window and looked at me through narrowed eyes.

"Yeah, yeah". I shook my head. "So, what are we waiting for? Let's get to this refugee camp thing already. It's getting stuffy in here".

"We have to wait for Danny". A small voice spoke out. I didn't notice Sam nestled between Nika and Evan in the back. She had her head on her knees, arms wrapped around her legs. A curtain of light brown hair covered her face.

"Danny?" I asked.

"Her brother, he's supposed to meet us outside once we returned". Evan answered for her.

"How would he know you guys got back?"

"We planned to go out yesterday, and told him that we would be back around ten". He looked at the silver watch on his left wrist. Oh, I didn't notice that before.

"We're a little early. But in the mean time let's hang in here until then". He sat back in his seat, dragging a hand through his hair.

The muscles in his arms stretched the white shirt, the scene did weird fluttery things to my stomach. Elise coughed bringing me out of my stupor.

I shook my head.

"How long have you guys been in this refuge?" Elise asked them.

"Hm, it actually started off as a small group. Me, Sam, Danny, Tony and a couple others just scavenging the nearby towns for supplies. Then we came across this area. We decided to settle down here, make it our base. The amount of skine aters wasn't too much, we were able to clear the place of em'. Then more people joined our group and boom, it turned into a refuge".

That's impressive.

125

"How did people find youguys? Did they just walk around this area and end up with you or did you broadcast you're location?"

Elise asked. She turned in her seat and was facing me, her head laid against the driver's side window.

"This area's a little remote compared to the city, so we got a few survivors checking the place out. We tried to broadcast ourselves on the radio but, the frequencies shot, can't hear nothing but static".

I hate how relaxed Evan is. Honestly, he's got one hot bod that should have been featured in a World's Hottest Man magazine.

But, does her trust us this much? Tolead us to a refuge and he just met us? Suspicious. Or maybe I'm too paranoid for my own good.

"How many people are in your group?" Nika asked him. I could tell Evan was having an effect on her too. Did he notice the gleam of interest in her eyes? And the fact that she was checking him out...and not very discreetly. Elise may be the only one immune to his charms. I applaud her internally.

"About thirty of us, mostly men than woman". He looked at me and smirked. "Word of advice, you might want to be weary around them. Everyone's a little jumpy nowadays and you three are packin' a lot of heat; especially you jade". He gestured to the two katanas by my feet.

"I don't need your advice. I know how to look after myself. So do Elise and Nika. Like I said before, we won't cause any trouble unless you give us a reason to". I crossed my arms and glared at him. His smile grew, showing perfectly straight teeth. His storm gray eyes bore into mine and lowered. I smiled back in mockery, but that too lowered when I realized where his eyeswere roaming.I forgetthat most of the time crossing my arms, was a terrible idea and that I should never ever do it around guys or anyone for that matter.

Ever since that time solong ago, I decided to grow apair andwear a deep V-neck t-shirt to school. I never wear V-necks. They reveal too much. And in this moment, a white tank reveals way more than a stupid V-neck. My arms gave more lift to my bosom than the ridiculously expensive bra would ever give. I'm well aware that I have a big chest. It's become a bit of a complex over the years, people tell me that they're jealous of my huge knockers and that I should be grateful for them. Well, I'm not grateful because, they get in the way of everything. Genetics is a biatch!

"Yes, You've told me this when we first met. But, I'm just warning you to be careful". He took a while to admire the view and looked back up at me. Blasted, I wanna wipe that smile right off his face so badly!

"Are you done?" I asked him, and gave him a stern look.

"What do you mean?"heasked back. I paused and took a deep breath. You are calm, you are relaxed, and you will not stab this son of a biatch in the gut.

"Nothing". I muttered under my breath. I wasn't about the get into with him. I don't need more people to argue with about things. The list is getting long.

"Oh, look!" Nika was up against the window, pointing at the building in front of us. I squinted my eyes towards it. I was only able to pick out two silhouettes. They began walking to us, I tensed for a moment thinking they were Bodies, when they got closer my grip on the katana loosened. I sighed out in relief. The two men were tall, they strode with a sureness that made me a little on edge. I hate people like that sometimes, they appear arrogant and arrogance sometimes meets the ends of my fists. The truck shakes bellow me, the sound of a door slamming shut, Sam is sprinting half way to them and attacks the man to the left. They embrace for a while, the man pats her head with comfort.

"Break the truck door why don'cha". I grumbled. Evan snickered behind me and eased open the door, he took care to shut it as slowly as possible. When the thing clicked shut I groaned loudly and placed my head in my hands.

"What's wrong with you?" Elise asked. There was a blandness in her tone that I didn't like very much.

"Nothing's wrong!" I snarled.

"I beg to differ". Nika giggled back. My head throbbed at the temples as I massaged them. Anymore of this and my fevers gonna rise

"I haven't seen you act like that ever since you're teen boy band phase". Ooh, Elise was enjoying every minute of my pain wasn't she? Like every other crazed hormonal girl in her early teens, I went through a boy band phase. Yes, I was one of those people that liked to stick up posters of boy bands all over their walls and fantasize about them. Ew, the very memory makes me want to puke my guts out.

"That was then, and this is now". I said back. She shot me a confused glance and shrugged.

"I gotta admit, I was surprised we ran into them. And even more surprised with Evan. I was sweating all over the entire time.

I thought I was gonna faint". She then proceeded to fan herself with her hand.

"You and me both E. I wasn't sure I was gonna make it out alive". I chocked on a laugh when she snorted.

"Oh! And you Jade, It was like you both were battling each other mentally. I was waiting for one of you to give in and have at it". I stared at her mortified.

"And what do you mean by 'have at it'?" She wasn't suggesting... "Youguys practically had sex with your eyes, it was both funny and unpleasant to watch". Nika responded for her. My eyes widened and Elise collapsed onto the armrest. I was momentarily paralyzed.

"Oh god look at your face! C'mon jade, don't tell me you didn't just ealize it?" She shook as she tried to calm her self down enough to wait for my answer. I shook my head slowly.

"What? Oh—but...what do you mean by—what?" I babbled.

Pretty sure my face was as red as a tomato by now.

"Goodgod,you'refreakin adorable!" Elise wiped her eyes and sat up. "Each time you looked at him you had this face that said, 'I just met you but I wanna take you down and do indecent things together right here... right now', it took all of me not to laugh at you're sorry arse!"

"I so did not!" I screamed back.

"You totally did dude. You weren't the only one though, I was looking at him and he had his own face that said, 'I only met you just now but I wanna ravish you day and night, anywhere, everywhere, anytime', I never thought I'd live to see that kind of expression...like ever". Nika was laughing along with Elise. I had no words, I didn't know what to say or think. Since when? And how does having sex with your eyes even look like?

"No! Both of you just shut up!" I stomped the trucks floor.

"Don't deny it Jade". Elise droned out. She pat my knee and continued laughing. I swear one day, when she gets herself a guy I'm gonna ruin every chance they get with each other. I curse thee!

"Hey guys..." Nika stopped and poked us both, she pointed out her finger to the window and we both leaned towards it. Evan, Sam and I guess Danny and another man stood waiting by a wired gate. I pressed the button to rolldown thewindow and was immediately hit by a dry heat wave. I could feel my hair frizzing up already, fantastic!

Evan waved at me, signaling us to get out and follow them. I just wanted to forget about meeting him and drive off but... "I think it's time to go". Elise said to me. I looked at her and nodded. But I don't wanna!

"I'm excited". Nika was the first to go, she opened the door and hopped out.

"At least someone seems to be having fun". I groaned and opened the door. Once my boots hit the ground I wanted to dash back inside. The truck was cooler since the air conditioner was left on, and the sudden transition into the heat made me sway forward a little. I managed to right myself by leaning against the door.

"You alright?" Elise rounded the Hummer and stood beside me, hands still in front of me in case I fell forward.

"Yeah, just a little light headed. Let's get this shiznit over with". She raised an eyebrow at me and waited. I reached into the truck and took out both katanas. I told Elise to pop the trunk so I can get the back straps for them. Once that was done, I secured the leather straps across my chest and waist. Elise helped place the two swords in the back and tied them down. The weight of them both made me tilt back an inch, but before Elise could notice I shook out of it.

We didn't have to worry about the truck getting stolen because, from what she told me, Evan told her to park in the back. We were surrounded by red bricked walls and thick wired fences. They must have gotten out and unlocked the first gate to get inside. I was too out of it to care.

130

"Got everything?" Nika skipped back to us. Knitting picks hung loosely around her waist. She also had a metal bat behind her back. Elise was decked out too, ready to go.

"Ready Freddy". Elise sang. Shut. Up. She started forward with Nika at her tail. My body refused to follow...sodid my mind. With what took determination and skillI placed one foot in front of the other.

"This is gonna suck so much". And not one person could say otherwise.

Chapter 16

While we trailed behind, I took the time to look at my   surroundings. Inside the wired fence two red bricked buildings stood tall and ominous, casting shadows in every corner. The dry wind howled against them. I hate old buildings like this, they make me anxious. And anxious a Jade is not good for anyone. The area might've been an old factory. Better to find out then wait I suppose.

"This place gives me the creeps". Elise was shivering slightly next to me. She had one arm wrapped around mine and the other pressed against her chest. *Oh yeah, she's not good with eerie stuff like this...* "You okay there?" I asked, trying to hide my smile.

"S-sure..." Her large green eyes darting left and right. Perhaps checking to make sure the shadows weren't following after us.

"If you say so...Oh my god what's that?!" We both jumped at the same time, hers more exaggerated. She shrieked and spun in all directions, trying to find the cause of what spooked us. I doubled over laughing,my hand tryingto suppress the snort that exploded from my nose.

"What?" She stood there, staring at me in shock.

"Blasted! That was funny". I looked up at her and raised a brow. "And what were you planning to accomplish by using the bat like that?" She looked at me and down. She was holding the barrel of the bat, with the end of it sticking up. I'm not sure that's how you're supposed to hold it either. I slapped my hands together and she flinched backwards. My brow went evenhigher.

"That wasn't funny! What if those things heard me? What then?" She flipped the bat right side up and tucked it back behind her. It never lasts... "Then...we would end therotten mongrels before they'd even get within two feet of us". She shook her head andhuffed.

"Whatever". She turned and caught up with the rest of the group. Meanwhile, I tried to shake off whatever residue of laughter I had left in me. I needed to stay focused once inside. No time for fooling around. If they had a leader to their refuge then I would have to question them or Elise would.

I was walking next to Nika when we finally made it inside the compound. Cool air greeted us at the front, and I looked up. Large fans swung clockwise above us. They still have electricity.

"This is the center area of the building". Evan told us. The room was as big as the cafeteria room at our old school. I'd say about a half of a regular foot ball field. Tall windows stretched high against the walls. Some patched up with tape and cardboard.

"What was this building before everything happened?" Nika asked.

"When wefirstfound it, there werehuge machinesin the back.

I found cartridges of ink scattered on the flooring next to them.

I'd guess it was an ink printing facility. Couldn't be sure".

Random tables were pushed against the walls. Paper maps lie on them haphazardly. Chairs scattered all over the room. A few whiteboards here and there, with blackmarker written allover it. They've been busy.

"What's this you got here, Evan?" A gruff voice echoed from the other side of the room. Nika tensed beside me, both of her hands tucked into her pockets. Elise looked over her shoulder at me, she shrugged and stepped back over to my other side.Westood there sidebyside. I tried to appear casual, by relaxing my shoulders and crossing my arms. Putting more

134

weight on my left leg so that I'd lean a little. Nice and easy.

I'm not sure what surprised me more but, this man...he was practically towering over Evan. He might've been at least six foot five and then some. And it terrified the heck out ofme!

Not only was his height a great big woo-ha to me, his posture was disciplined, trained, cruel. For all it was worth, I have to admit this man who appears to be in his late forties and could possibly stand as my father...
he looked good. "Men who age well, are good men" what mom wouldn't give to see this giant in person? Perhaps he was in the military, a retired veteran.

Long powerful arms were placed on his hips. He was oddly fascinating to look at. His decent physic due to constant exercise and heavy lifting. His age showing from the deep lines on his narrow face. He had a generous cloud of short dark hair with streaks of silver at his temples. His skin was a shade darker than mine.

But of course, I was a bit pale for my tastes. I was what they call "Caramel" skinned. And if that's light, this guy was my opposite. I don't wanna be that dark, I'll look...strange. Thanks to my African American and Filipino heritage I was a bit different than the normal mix. My mom's told me I also have a bit of European Spanish in my blood. 'You're great-great grandmother was from Spain...you have a little bit of everything'. Yep, a little bit of freakin everything.

Why don't we add Native American, from my father's side to the mix as well? I'm like a freaky multi-mixedhybrid.

During my time alone—talking to myself—the room grew quiet.

Like, a silence too blasted quiet, that it made me shiver slightly. I slapped myself mentally, and looked to my right.

Elise had the funniest expression on her face. Bright emerald orbs blinked back at me. I quirked an eyebrow at her in amusement. She hissed out a breath and punched me in the ribs.

"Ow! Jesus, what's your problem?" I snarled back at her, clutching my ribcage. That's gonna turn into a big beautiful bruise.

"D'you really think its okay to zone out at a time like this?" For a minute there I swear I could have seen flames puffing out of her nose. You're a Dragon Elise.

"I zoned out?" I asked her, my voice caught at the end. My ribs were still aching. She huffed out a long breath and clicked her tongue.

"No, it's perfectly natural to stand there with your eyes unblinking for atleast five minutes, mouth slightly open, and not answering when someone is talking to you—shouting—at you to reply".

She leaned back to glare at me.

"I'm not sure if any of that was sarcasm...or you were being serious". I asked nonchalantly.

"Oh for the love of- Yes! Jade. You zoned out...again. What have I been telling you for the past couple years? You need to fix that shiznit real quick, I hate it when you do that. It's both concerning and annoying". He voice pierced the wide room. The echo bouncing off the stone walls.

"Would it hurt you to pay attention for at least a couple minutes?" she asked.

I shrugged and gave her an innocent look.

"Can't help it, sorry". She stared at me silently for a minute, then she whipped out the metal bat and posed as if she were going to attack me with it. Green eyes burning with fury.

"I'll tell ya what you can'thelp..." She muttered under her breath.

I was too distracted by her sudden burst of rage, to see the silver gleaming bat before it made contact with my head. I ducked down in time, and rolled to the side. I couldn't help butchuckle.

"E, girl, you gotta calm down". I put my hands up in surrender.

She turned to me, her lips pulled back in a snarl. And I thoughtI had anger issues... "You calm down!" She swung the bat down, and I dodged to the right. My knees skinning the rough ground.

"That doesn't even make sense...I am calm". I crouched on the ground. My katanas held back in their guard. Blasted, she was smok- ing. Her face was red and she circled me with slow even steps.Her breathing harsh. Don't tell me she's PMS'ing... "You don't make sense—and stay still while I—Blasted, stay still!" She jumped towards me, aiming for my head the entire time. She swung left and right, in every way trying to damage my head. My head!

"If I stay still I'll get myself killed". I told her. Pissed. That's the only word I found worthy for her actions. And the reason? Just because I zoned out during our meet and greet with these people.

I didn't even know I was the one supposed to talk. That's why there's two of us. If for whatever reason I am unable to speak, she's there to substitute for me. I have the right to zone out when I feel like it!

"Good". She growled out. Making one more lunge for me. I crouched there, awaiting my punishment. Seconds past and I felt no pain. My eyes were sealed shut, I opened one lid slowly and muffled a giggle. Nika was standing in front of me, one arm shot out encircling the metal bat. Her expression neutral. I coughed to hide my laugh and stood up, brushing the dirt from my knees. I looked down at them, and found them both bleeding slightly.The skin red around the wounds. I'm gonna need to patch those up... "You good?" I asked Elise over Nikas shoulder. She seemed okay now, I guess swinging the bat all over the place, allowed her to lose some steam. She snatched the bat back from Nikas grip and tugged it behind her. With a heavy sigh, she turned to the...holy! Unaware of our surroundings, while we were fighting a small crowd had gathered about the room. I'd say around thirty or so people in all gawked back at us. I looked back at Elise and grimaced. She had on that freaky 'All is well' smile on her face.

A mask of extreme control strained her features that I took notice. Everyone else thought differently...they weren't up close to see the corner of her mouth twitching.

"Sure". She paused at looked to me. "Are you?" Seriously, even if that face promised divine punishment I had to stifle another laugh. I'll leave that to the latter.

"Yep, tis all good in the hood". I shot my own personal 'All is freakin well' smile at her. We'll talk later Standford...just you wait.

Someone cleared their throat and I turned back to the crowd. Mostly men than women...all of them looked weary. I have to remember to ask Evan if I could check some of them. I'd hate for someoneto beinfectedwithout our knowledge. I'mnot evensure anyone of these people has seen someone go through the change. It's a disturbing thing, ever since that time in the bathroom stall... Still haunts my dreams I can tell you that.

Chapter 17

The room was fully crowded by the next hour. The air suddenly felt stuffy.

Breath Jade, you're cool, you're cool I remained close to Nika and Elise. Both their expressions unreadable.

"This is...those are a lot of people". Elise tapped the cool metal bat secured behind her back.

"There could be more, the entire facility ground is large enough the shelter at least a hundred or more. I mean, from what I could see when we first entered". Her voice barely in a whisper, I looked to her and nodded in agreement.

"Yeah, but so far I'm seeing only thirty or so-". The crowd's murmurings became louder. The shuffling of feet made me tense. For no reason at all I'm starting to feel a bit edgy. I hate crowds.I hate large groups of people, especially in confined places. Just the image of so many packed into one room made me extremely anxious. The ceiling fans didn't help to comfort me, goose bumps raised on my skin. I inhaled, and withdrew a shaky breath slowly between my lips. Nika nudged me with her elbow.

"You alright? Youlook pale". Her brows furrowed with worry. I cleared my throat and nodded.

"I'm just tired—as surprising as that sounds—and I'd like to get this over with before I finally lose it".

The lines between her brows deepened, her stare felt like an eternity. Before I could respond, Evan walked up to me. His features were schooled. Storm gray eyes locked on mine. What?

"As youcan see,our people are abitrestless.AndInoticed that you've been oddly quiet for a good while".

I said nothing. A grin broke out on his face. I couldn't help myself, my eyes lowered just slightly, my attention on those lips of his. I noticed that his lower lip was fuller than the other. I could image him pouting, protruding its fullness...it looked tasty from my point of view.

What I wouldn't give to bite that sucker!

"I want the people to feel at ease while you're all around them. I would be grateful if you'd allow me to keep you're weapons...for the duration of your stay I mean".

My attention snapped back up to his eyes. The grin was still there Blasted! How distracting. I gaped at him. "Pardon?"

"You have to understand that the people here, they're a bit... jumpy. A few have children, and we don't want people walking around them with sharp objects. It's dangerous for them". He said. I crossed my arms again, and cocked myhead. Surely he must be joking?

"I see. But, we can just hide them from sight. The purpose for having our weapons gives us security," He didn't respond, so I continued. "Besides, what if we're to be attacked? I'd like to have my weapons at the ready whenever I'd need them". I smirked.

"Plus, confiscating my babies wouldn't change a thing, it'd pain me to part with them".

The storm in his eyes darkened. My skin tingled, and I wondered whether that was in warning or in anticipation. My hands twitched.

You gonna fight me for it big guy?

"I'd takethatas a'no' then?" He chuckled, his darklocks swaying across his forehead. Twitch.

"That's right. I have every right to keep them. If you don't like it, well...that's too bad".

We went at it. Glaring at one another. He shifted closer, and I had to crane my neck back to look up at him. His eyes narrowed, I was pretty sure he had the perfect view of the tops of my bosom.

I keep forgetting that crossing my arms is like begging for people to notice em'!

My white tube tank top had slid down during my fight with E.

My fingers itched to pull the top up to cover thembetter.

No, if I did that he'd know that I noticed his looking...and that'd be askin' for it!

"Do you want me to take them from you myself?" His voice was deeper than earlier. My nose mere inches from his chin. He lowered his head, when he did that my god! Two inches... his lips were two inches from mine and I felt every warm breath.

Not good! So not good!

My knees suddenly felt like freakin Jell-O. I should lean, gives us both some space. But I couldn't move. I'm like, practically screaming at my own body.

Move!

"Try". My voice barely came out in a murmur. My mouth suddenly felt dry and it took me a while to swallow correctly.

I dare you bro!

I was hardly aware of our very uneasy if not curious audience. I heard Nika's and Elise's boots scuffle behind me. His grin grew into a wide smile. Straight white teeth shot back at me.

I returned it with a close lipped smile. It probably looked more like a grimace.

I hate attractive men. He made no move. After what felt like forever he chuckled and backed up. I let out a frustrated sigh when he was a good couple feet away from me. He began talking to the giant. His dark amber eyes flicking up towards me a few times. I felt a jab between my shoulder blades. I spun on my heel, and flinched.

To be perfectly honest, even people like me are afraid of a few things. I'm afraid of large bodies of water, and spiders. But, nothing could have scared me more than the sight in front of me.

"W-what?" Stuttering is yet another fault of mine. Ihate itwith a burning passion. These idiots were...what's the word to define this? Smirking? No, far worse. They both had on the most terrifyingly goofy expressions on their faces. Mirrored, thin lips stretched across their faces. Teeth flashing. Perhaps with a bit more force, the corner soft heir mouths would rip. Their eyes gleaming, and both shockingly bright. Pupils dilated to complete tiny black dots in orbs of emerald and orange flecks.

There they were, my two idiots, looking at me as if I'd somehow discovered some long lost treasure. As if I'd done something amazing. Amazingly stupid. Nika started to laugh. Or more like cackle. Squeaks between breaths. I shuddered again and her laugh got louder. Elise spoke first, "Well, if I didn't know any better—I would have set you two up from the very beginning". She leered, which was very, very disturbing!

"I have no idea what you're talking about". My arms clutching my sides defiantly. She tsked and poked my nose.

"Silly, silly, girl. Who are you trying to fool? I was right behind you. I've witnessed all of it". She flicked my nose again, and giggled. My brows lowered.

"Touch my nose again... see what happens". I snarled. She ignored my warning and pinched my cheeks next. Sighing she said,

"You know, at first I thought. 'We don't have time for guys or any of that crap. We've got more pressing issues to deal with than a simple romance. And that, we are in the middle of what could possibly be a worldwide zombie apocalypse—which, by the way I knew would happen one day—doesn't mean you can't go hunting every once in a while". She gave me a look and ceased her pinching. Her hands moved to my shoulders and gave them a heavy slap.

"Hunting?" I asked. She nodded slowly and purred.

"Yes jade, hunting. You are now the predator in this wild hunt. The world is filled with worthy prey". She smirked, her lashes fluttering. "I see that you've already got something in your sights..."

"I'm not sure where this conversation is heading".

"Jade," She shook my shoulders lightly. "You were both doing that eye-sexing thing again". She took a moment to fan herself.

"Cause holy cow! I and Nika weren't even sure that we could have intervened to get both of your guys' attention.I haven't seen something like that...like, ever! Something like that only exists in young adult romance novels—and I know you know what I'm talking about—because, it got way too hot for my comfort...did you even notice youguys were pressed up against eachother —oh my god! I felt like I was imposing on a possible make out scene and I didn't know whether to cover my eyes or...or...gah!" I blinked. Elise was rambling...she had the serious case of verbal diarrhea.

"E. We've had this talk before. You know I can't-".

"C'mon admit it! You're totally into him. I know it's not like loveat-first-sight kind of into him...but," She shook her head. "This is a once in a life time chance opportunity! When are you ever gonna meet someone like him? I'm pretty sure half the population's been eaten by undead Monsters; you have to take this chance Jade!"

She was shouting at me, but just quiet enough for only me to hear. I stared at her in awe. She's always been the one trying to keep me away from boys (Correction: Men) always telling me to wait for the right guy, never flirt with random dudes. It startled me.

The fact that she's pushing me towards Evan...A dude who we've just met, and probably three years my senior. She wants me to hook up with him? Or something?

Before I could respond, Nika slammed into my side.

"You gonna hit him up or wha?" Her goofy face plastered on.

"She's gonna do more than 'hit him up' if you catch my drift".

Elise winked at Nika. They both giggled. I groaned.

"No one's hitting anyone up!" I shoved my hands in my hair and pulled the strands, I tried to cover my face with them; my face heating up from the embarrassment.

"And the sky ain't blue". Nika said.

"And the grass ain't green". Elise chirped back. Besides tormenting me with their ridiculousness, they looked happy. Better even, Nika was a lot more energetic now and that made me smile.

Having to fight our way to survive takes a whole lot out of a person, hopefully our time here will allow us to relax. Still, I've been itching to slice something for a while now. I wonder if they spar here.

I looked up and found the burly giant Evan was talking to in front of me. He smiled down at me with an ease that made me a little...jittery. He probably meant the smile to comfort me. His size didn't help the ease either. I looked up at his hard amber eyes. Mine were close to the same shade, except mine were a darker hazel which, lightened in the sunlight. I met his smile with my own. We had one of those silent conversations. After a moment he nodded, and I nodded back.

"Welcome, the names Jason. Pleasure meetin' ya". His tenor voice reverbe rated down to my core. I shivered in voluntarily, just slightly hoping Nika and Elise wouldn't notice.

"Likewise, I'm Jade". I gestured to Nika and Elise. Nika twitched.

"Nika". She said quietly.

"You can call me Elise, not Eli...don't like the nick-name. Elise is just fine". She had her hands on her hips, arrogance oozing from every pore. I snickered and shook my head. Jason stared down at her a bit longer than looked to me. I straightened my spine, in his presence I felt like I had to appear dominant, tough.

He nodded again, amber eyes sparkling with...excitement? I wasn't sure what that meant. But right now, I had to focus on the now.

No zoning out!

I justhoped that I gave a good impression...and that I wouldn't vomit on the floor in front of so many people.

Chapter 18

There's a wonder to be hold, especially when you're in the middle of a crowd. Everyone's talking all at once, and I feel like my heads gonna peal right off my shoulders. My body was restless.

I really, really, needed to slice something up. Anything! Just something to ward off the tension in my muscles. My eyes darting left and right, trying to sight out a gap in between the crowds cluster.

Elise was beside me, this time she was the one doing the talking. I didn't trust my voice at the moment. Nika was sitting on one of the chairs that she pulled up. One leg was pulled up, her arm was wrapped around the knee. The other dangled, occasionally swinging back at forth. I spotted a few stares from the others around us.

Some of them gawked atthe twin katanas on myback. Iwanted to unsheathe them and show them off just to get a reaction.

"How long have you guys been out there? It's just the three of you right, were there any others in your group before?" Jason asked.

This was the interrogation part of our meeting. I'm not totally okay with talking to adults dead on like Elise so, she's the boss of the hour. I leaned a hip against the table we were standing around. Evan was... somewhere. I'd lost him a couple minutes ago. I cocked my head to the side, trying to appearlax.And at the same time aware.

"I'm not exactly sure how long we've been out there. I'd guess about half a month or so. And no, it's just us". She jerked her chin towards me and Nika. "Funny thing was, we had this plan that we'd written down a few years back. We just, wrote down ideas and plans—which worked out fairly well—just in case something like this were to occur. I know,it sounds weird but, we were paranoid about stuff like that. Though, don't take this the wrong way.

We didn't ask for something like this to happen. The situation totally sucks". She took a moment to let that settle in.

Yeah, we are zombie freaks. Paranoids; crazy SOBs that had no idea what we were asking. It was very likely to happen one of these days. I admit, when the world went to shiznit I got a little excited.

Albeit, I was freaked the freak out about the suddenness of the shiznit storm that rolled into our lives. We had everything down into great detail. Where to go, which sections of the city to stay clear from. Prioritizing is key, I'm sure that without our plan, we'd have died the second night. Although, Elise had this little thing about a possible alien invasion—she thought it'd benefit us all that making a plan for something like that was a good idea. I didn't say anything then. And I won't say anything now.

Jason eyed me keenly, the humor in his eyes still evident. What?

I scowled inwardly. You keep eying me old man, and I'll remove you're sight in two seconds flat!

"Elise is doing a good job. Huh". Nika whispered next to me. I peeked at Elise, her posture was straight, and her answers were smooth. As if she rehe arsed the lines before. Although, what no one else noticed, was the tip of her right booted toe tapping lightly on the ground.

Unless you're really, really looking. The tapping gets faster the more Jason questions her.

"Sure...give it five minutes and she'll ask to switch". Nika smirked and hid her snicker. Surprisingly enough, after six minutes she asked if I could answer in her stead.

"Jade was the one in the front lines most of the time. She's a bit more specific—I'm sure she'll be able to answer you better than I". She stood up and thumped my shoulders with her hands. I raised a brow when she stared at me pleadingly.

"I thought you said you had everything in control?" I asked her. She tilt forward to whisper.

"The heck I did! I underestimated the dude's power. Every time he stares at me with those death rays he calls eyes, I shuddered...shuddered! In fear Jade!"

I made an effort to mask my amusement. The corners of lips twitching from the strain. I nodded instead and reassured her that I'll take it from here. I walked around her and plopped into the chair. I crossed my legs and leaned my forearms on top of the table in front of me.

"If you don't mind me answering you're questions instead of her, you may proceed to do so". I clasped my hands together

and waited. Both his brows rose up. I may not have as much selfconfidence as Elise does but, a guy like this—I won't be intimidated so easily.

Partially... "Eh, I don't mind at all. In fact, I'd like to ask you a more specific question. If you can answer it truthfully". I wasn't sure if he meant to say that as a question.

"Have at it". I drummed the wooden surfaces with my fingers. "How many have you killed?" He asked. All humor vanished. I heard a few people gasp. Some held their breaths. Why must they act this way? "I don't know," I shrugged. "I don't count the dead when they fall to my feet". The people behind Jason stiffened. Interesting. "Estimation?" He inquired.

"I'd say around thirty or more...counting the few we ran over withourtruck—thatmakesthirty-fivemaybe,"Ishruggedagain.

"Why does it matter?"

"In total or just yourself?" He asked without answering my question. I cocked my head to the other side and sat up. Ah, he wantsto see if I'm a hazard to his group. I guess it's normal to question a person they've just met about the amount of kills they made.

Considering my age and gender and all that jazz... I wonder, does he think I'm dangerous? A liability?

"Just myself? Hm..." I paused and grinned. "Truthfully, I've decapitated two of those things. The rest either sliced by my swords or bashed in by baseball bats". All noise in the room went silent. Perhaps my answer surprised them. I watched his face for any physical changes. I found it funny how half of the crowd looked disgusted and the other in wonder. The disgusted half are probably debating whether or not they could trust someone like me to be around them. Or their children. Good. Cause, I don't quite trust anyone here either. Not like I really care though. Jason grunted, that seemed to settle the people down. I felt a hand on my shoulder and turned my head to lookup. Elise leaned down to whisper in my ear.

"I think their impressions of you startled them—which is not good. You need them to trust us—you". Her hand gripped my shoulder, short nails bit into my skin causing me to grimace inwardly. I chuckled.

"I know.But he asked me to answer him truthfully. I am a woman of her word, I tell no lies". When needed.

"You could have been a bit more discreet". I'm gonna have half crescent moon shaped bruises on my shoulder tomorrow.

Oh boy!

"Being discreet isn't really my thing ya know. Besides, discretion is now but a luxury in our thoroughly fudged up world E.

And I have the habit of being quite descriptive". I said lightly.

"Discretion would be a wise luxury to be using now since there are children in this room, and people who might not even know what the heck is going on out there". She lifted her hand away, and backed up. I'll take that as a warning then. Jason stared at me curiously. I gave him my widest smile. His broad shoulders twitched.

"I'm curious, where did you get those?" He gestured with his chin towards my back. My smile broadened with pride, I lifted my chin.

"Those good sir, are the shining stars of our little band of misfit's.

I'm proud to say that, without my babies I probably wouldn't have never made it out in the world," I paused "Of course I would have been like a chicken who's heads been chopped off if I didn't have Nika or Elise by my side as well".

"Right on". Nika and Elise both hollered.

"I see, I won't ask how you came across those swords but, I will ask... what will you're purpose be now that you're here?" His expression still as stone. I lifted my shoulders.

"Depends. We didn't plan on finding other survivors like you guys. But, you did save us the trouble of finding shelter. For that we are grateful". I nodded to him. I'm not usually this formal, but when I need to...'formal Jade comes out'.

Chapter 19

Icould say the same.

It was a good blasted thing you came across Evan and his group, even with our losses," He lowered his head grimly "You managed to bring everyone else back safely". Oh, about that... "Would you like to know the cause of their deaths?" I asked. He frowned and shook his head.

"No need. Samantha had already told me everything. Tony was a good man, and Dean might've been a bit weak on the outside, but he was bright kid". He sighed and scratched the back of his head "Should have never gone out that way, they didn't deserve at death like that". I would have expressed my condolences, but that's not how I am. Death happens. If you get bit, or caught... you're done. There's no reset button. Ain't no one got three lives? Finished.

"Regarding that issue. Is there anyone in your group ill?" I asked. That seemed to get his full attention. I gave him a moment to think.

"Not that I know of—no. Why do you ask?" Weariness detected in his tone.

"Before Dean..." I looked to the crowd and sighed. "When he attacked us, he wasn't well. I saw no indication—from what I could see—of any bites on him".

"I didn't see anything like that before he left". He narrowed his eyes in thought. He leaned back to ask the people behind him.

When he turned back to me, his expression was serious.

"No one else had noticed any faults with Dean. Although..." his eyes strayed from my face to somewhere behind me. I felt the hairs on my neck rise, a looming shadow past above me. I told myself to stay calm; don't turn around. It's fine, just relax, you're good... totally good.

"He was acting strangely during our stock run a few days ago".

His presence was—something! I shook myself mentally. Evans voice sounded A LOT closer than I would'vepreferred.

"Strange how?" Jason asked him.

"He...he was always a twitchy kid, but yesterday he was-". He cleared his throat. "He looked, well...he didn't look good. He kept tellin' us he was fine. Tony thought otherwise". Jason nodded. I felt his warm hand grip the back of the chair. The plastic creaking under the pressure.

"He was shivering so blasted much, his skin was like, a sickly gray. Then the next thing we knew he just..." I don't know why but, I wanted to comfort him somehow. I could tell these people were as close as family. He didn't get into the details about how Dean changed, no the suddenness. Form what I could gather, the amount of time it takes to change varies from the bite amount and infection start time. Depending on how long ago the bite was. In that stall...it happened so fast—too fast.

I couldn't distinguish her bites from the amount of blood she had on her body. Her blood or "Theirs". Evan was still close behind me, I was well aware of his every move. Please move I beg of you!

"I would suggest sir that you or the others could take the time to check those who've recently been on a run. From bites to scratches. I would assume that blood-on-blood contact is the main transmission of the infection". He regarded me coolly, then grunted in agreement. I think that's his thing, "grunting".

"Sounds like a good plan". He then stood from his seat and started to bark out orders to the few around him. They scattered like ants and went separate ways. He turned and walked towards me in only three large strides.

"As much as I trust you now; have you too checked yourselves for bites or scratches?" He crossed his muscled arms and stared down at me. I looked up and grinned.

"I assure you sir, I and my friends have taken good care to check ourselves constantly—daily even—we are very cautious people.

You don't have to worry about endangering you're people". My formality biting back with a vengeance. I blame those pesky—yet intriguing—old time romance novels I used to read. Sooner or later I might even let a bit of brogue slip out. Curse you Scott's and you're hot, hot accents!

The corners of his mouth curled up slightly at my words. 'Tis all good fun.

"Alright. Then, with that we are done with our talk. I trust you three enough as is. But as a fair warning, if any of you slips up, shows any distrust or puts my people in danger," He stepped closer and stared down at me. If this man were trying to scare the pants off of me...he's already succeeded.

"I'd have the pleasure of tossing you're arsesout of this building without your weapons. Is that understood?"

"Yes sir". I stood up slowly and gave him a light salute. He turned and walked away. Right when I turned on my heel, I smacked my foreheadwith Evanschin. Shivering, I hopped back and glared at him.

"Blasted woman, you have a hard head. Is it made of brick or something?" He grimaced and rubbed his chin. Even with the scowl on his face, humor sparkled in his storming eyes.

"Granite.And if youweren't so freaking close you wouldn't have hurt yourself now would you?"

"Granite?" He chuckled. "I like that you don't even deny that fact. I guess I wasn't paying as much attention as I should have been". He shook his head, making those blasted freaking dark locks of his flutter; it just keeps distracting me! Makes me wanna shove my hands over his hair just to pull it back— Wait... "It's genetic so I can't help it". I turned away before he could reply. Elise and Nika were right there. That goofy expression forever glued on their faces.

"Your faces are gonna get stuck like that". I grumbled.

"Jade-" Elise started. I grabbed her jaw and shook it lightly.

"We are not gonna start this conversation again E. Have I made myself clear?" She blinked those bright green eyes at me and nodded. I released my hold and shoved by hands in the pockets of my jean shorts. They both stood silently, await- ing my orders. I guess that's what it looks like from another per- son's perspective.

I sighed heavily, and perked my chin up. I shot them both a wide smile.

"Now that that's over...what do you wanna do?" I asked them. They eyed me, pondering my question. Nika clapped her hands together like a five-year old on sugar high. Elise tilted her head back and yawned.

"I'm tired as heck, I'm gonna take a nap. You'll find me— somewhere". She turned and skipped off. I looked to Nika, she raised her hands and shrugged.

"Don't ask me, I don't read minds". I pursed my lips.

"Mhm".

"Okay...if that's all I'm gonna...check the place out. See ya!" I was then left alone to wallow.

“Alrighty then, let’s see if they have a kitchen in this big arse building”.

Chapter 20

T he building interior was a whole lot bigger than I originally   thought. More grit matted windows stretched from the ground to the ceiling. I'd say from the bottom up, the building was fifty-sixty feet in width. I felt like I've been walking forever. The length of the grounds were uncertain.

Eventually, I started to pass handless iron doors. Some even looked wielded shut. Secret? Ooh I love secrets. The wide hallway was bright from the natural light spilling in from the windows. I tipped my head up and found light panels on the ceiling, someone had taken the time to hang small Christmas lights on the walls. The cheery multi-colored lights twinkled against the shadows. I felt no joy from seeing them.

I hummed under my breath. An old 90's song stuck in my head. Something about cheesy love and comparinghisfeelings to a roller coaster. I couldn't think of the blasted name. I allowed it to bother me for a while.

After about an hour walking through many barren hallways, I heard voices up ahead. Odd how I didn't find anyone walking in the hallways. The only sign of human life, was a few scraps of cloth or empty cans of soda. When was the last time I had a soda? I'd long to taste the sweet carbonated drink ever since shiznit went down. I wonder if they have some left. Perhaps a hidden stash. Maybe with enough skulking I can find it. A treasure hunt!

I half skipped—walked towards the voices. The rough heals of my boots scuffing the cemented flooring. I came to a stop in front of a set of double metal doors. Both were held open by hinge locks, warm air brushed against my skin. A familiar scent crawled its way into my senses—cinnamon. The steady aroma off resh baked bread. I sniffed, a stew was being prepared. The different scents were intoxicating, I had to still myself. Don't attack head first Jade! Have some control.

I peered into a medium set room. White tables lined the space, four in each row. The room can fit about fifty or so people. To one side held more windows, some purposely smashed open for air flow. Large ceiling fans spun lazily above the room. One large table was pushed against the wall. It had stacks of paper plates and plastic utensils. Everything looked so freakin organized, itnearly brought tears to my eyes. I wouldn't call myself a perfectionist, I just like it when things are in neat order. I have a habit of straightening things when they look crooked. My mom used to call me a neat freak. Although, I wouldn't classify as one since my room was normally trashed. I'm not sure how that made any sense. My room is messy yet, I go all clean freak psycho if a can of fruit was a few centimeters off kilter.

I did that at a store once. I was mistaken for an employee. It's happened at least too many times in my life time. I tipped toed into the room, hands lax at my sides. The scents got stronger the more I entered the room.

A section of the room, held a second room with a thick metal door on one side and the other was left open. The voices grew louder, the clanking of steal on steal added to the light bubbling of the stew. I felt my mouth water. It's been a long arse time since

I've eaten real food. I wouldn't count granola bars and pop-tarts as real food.

I popped my head in. I found the kitchen...score one for Jade!

It was one of those cafeteria kitchens. Large grills and double stacked ovens lined the end of the room. Sauce pans and skill let's cluttered half the stoves. Something sizzled and popped. Large stock fridges lined one wall across from the stoves. And in the middle sat a cluster of women at a wide wooden island.

It was stifling. A thin layer of sweat coated on my brows. The women at the table hadn't even noticed me yet. Non, non! You gotta be more aware than that. I hesitated in the door way, all of them had their backs to me. If I were an enemy, I'd take advantage of that and attack them while they're vulnerable. But, I'm not a bad person—unless you piss me off—and Elise told me to "Behave". I breathed in and out to calm my slightly reckless nerves. I knocked lightly on the door frame. The laughter died down. One of the ladies spun around in her seat and jumped at the sight of me. My brows shot up in question.

She was short, petite, with darkly tanned skin and a flurry of wild ebony curls bounced a top her head. She wavered for a second then gave me one of the most comforting smiles in the entire world! Dude...I feel pretty blasted chipper right now for some reason.

She could have been in her late thirties (My guess: 37)

Although she looked wayyy younger than that. Laugh lines and all that. The corners of her large dark hazel eyes creased. She had high cheek bones, each cheek complimented by deep set dimples.

The others at the table stared at me. One in particular...scowled fiercely. Problem? I'd deal with that later, in the mean while introductions are in order. I leaned my hip against the door frame and returned her smile with my own.

"Hecko".

"Hey! Looks like you found our kitchen". She had a bit of an accent and I couldn't pin point it. Her voice was higher than what I originally thought.

"Yeah, it took me a while...this place is like a labyrinth". I sighed. She giggled,

"Wegot lost the first couple of days. But, after a while we got used to it. I can probably walk around with my eyes closed now". Her laugh was hearty, making the mess of curls on her head jiggle.

"Good to know. If I get lost the next time I'll just rely on you guys for help then. Just call me 'slightly directionally challenged girl".

I chuckled nervously. Great Jade, just proves you're more of an idiot than they imagined.

Her dark eyes sparkled and she belted out another laugh. The other women—besides scowling girl—laughed right along with her. She was like a fudging ray of sunshine! Tooblasted bright for my night scoping eyes. Sunglasses...I needed sunglasses!

"My names Cathy or you can call me Cat. Whichever name you'd prefa," She gestured a hand towards the five other women. "The two on my right are Tyanna and Bradley," Bradley?

"At the edge are Sophia and Mag," They both gawked at me through wide eyes. They looked about my age, maybe farther... can't be sure.

"And little miss Tanni in the middle". She nodded towards the scowling girl—Tanni. She had waist length copper red hair that was pulled into a messy bun. (Again, just from a guessing look). Stray strands tumbled down her back, some stuck to her heat flushed face. Her dark green eyes narrowed down at me. Even with her stupidly small heart shaped face and thin pouted lips...she didn't seen cute at all. But I took the death glare she gave me full on. The corners of my lips twitched. Looks like I've made an enemy already.

"Great meeting you all. You can just call me Jade".

"Ooh, like the stone?" Tyanna asked. Her bob cut blond hair swayed.

"Yeah, I guess so. My mom never really told me her reason on why she picked it". I shrugged.

"Does that make you normally jaded then?" Tanni snorted. I cocked a brow at that and didn't reply.

"It's a lovely name. Better than mine I can give ya that". Bradley pipped. She had a hint of an Australian accent. Cool.

"Bradley is a good name. It's casual and fit's you nicely". Mag smacked her arm playfully. It looked painful. Mag was a bit heavy set. Her arms were thick, yet muscular. She had black pixiecut hair with static blue high lights. Her eyes the darkest I've ever seen of brown.

"Bradley is a boy's name! What would ya feel if you were called "Brad" during the first half of your middle school years? Addto the fact that I had short arse hair—I looked like a boy!" She slammed her fist on the counter top to make her point. Sophia jumped in her seat.

Meg snorted and shook her head.

"Eh? Language...why are you mad at me? I wasn't the one to name you, blame you're mother".

"Sounds like it sucked. Although I find it funny how you're named Bradley, while you're sis is named Sophia...I'm sensing favoritism in the family hm?"

Tyanna tsked. Sophia blinked and a blush crept up her cheeks. Right to the tips of her ears. Holy ghouls in October, she was freakin adorable! I'd guess she was a year or two younger than me, with baby blue eyes and thick dark lashes to back em' up. Her shoulder length wavy coffee hair framed a slim face. She rarely spoke, but she had a strange regal air around her. Her delicately pointed nose scrunched up in embarrassment. And I've never seen someone so blasted pale—beside Elise—she had a blemish free face. Ugh, beautiful people make me nervous as shiznit!

While in comparison to Bradley, she was tall for a women. Her sitting height surprised me. She had sharp blue eyes, a shade darker than Sophia's. Same face, but her strong jaw jutted out when she spoke. Her wispy coffee hair hitched into a tight pony tail. At least we had something in common: her brows sat low on her eyes making it look like she was glaring at everyone—everything.

I can't remember the last time someone asked me; "Why do you look so mad?" and I'd say, "I'm not mad". Then they'd say I was glaring. I can't help how my face looks. You want me to sew my brows up to look happy 24/7?

"Don't put Soph in the middle of this". She shot back at Mag. Sophia's face reddened more, and I was afraid she was gonna turn into a tomato.

"Alright girls that's enough", Cathy clapped her hands twice. "I think you've officially scared our new guest". She gestured towards me and I stiffened. I chuckled nervously.

"Don't worry about it. I've developed a heavy tolerance forthings like this". Tanni shot me the death glare over her shoulder. I don't really understand this girl. Does she scowl like that every time she meets someone new or what? I want to smack it right off her face, my fingers itch to unsheathe my katana. How about I carve that look into your face? You'll be a distant cousin to the Joker. I'm tempted to smile and ask her,

"Why so serious?"

"Well now that we've finished our introductions, would you like to help us make lunch? We've got one more spot left". Cathy slapped the wooden stool next to Tyanna. She turned around in her seat to fully face me. Tyanna had unusually deep blue eyes, yet as bright as a cornflower. They seemed to stand out on her light cocoa skin and blond bob cut hair. She bounced in her seat excitedly.

"C'mon, I'll show ya how we cut the veggies". I smirked and walked over to the table. She spun back around, while I placed my bottom on the cool wooden seat. I tried not to squirm at the closeness of their bodies around mine. Close quarters! Calm down Jade...you're good!

"Since we have only three cooking knives we pass them around like this". She slid the small cutting knife across the table to Mag. She picked it up by the handle cautiously and began to slice up a carrot. I eyed the sharp blade with interest. The steady thud of the blade cutting bits and pieces off the carrot. My throat made an odd growl that rumbled down to my chest. Oh good god...a carrot getting annihilated is making me feel all kinds of 'what the freak' right now! I'm blasted giddy even

Chapter 21

Iswallowed loudly. Tyanna stopped dicing the onion in her hands   and gave me a worried look.

"You okay?" She cocked her head to the side in thought. "This must be making you hungry huh? Don't worry. In about twenty minutes lunch should be out these doors in ajiffy". She continued to dice while she hummed.

"Here". Bradley rolled a couple Yukon potatoes over to me. I caught one that almost went off the edge; fast as lightning. I smiled inwardly. Those reflexes though... She stared at me curiously, then whistled low. She shook her head and got out a bag of green apples and started to cut them up. I wonder if they had raided a supermarket to get all this food. I held up a potato and twirled it slowly in myhand.

"These still look fresh. Where'd you get em'?" I asked examining it.

"About a couple weeks ago. Our last group of runners past by a farmers market. They said, some of the fruits and vegetables haven't gone spoiled yet, so they took what they could carry and brought it here". Mag explained.

"How convenient". I muttered. Mag looked up at me and smirked. "It was heck a convenient. The run before them onlycame back with boxes of microwavable food and gooey frozen TV dinner packages". She shivered and made a gagging sound.

"Yeah I've never seen so much half frozen meat loaf and peas in all my life". Bradley added. Sophia jerked her chin in silent agreement. She doesn't talk much does she? I won't ask though.

I ain't about to pry into her business; ain't nosy like some people. Tyanna wiped down the knife with cloth and handed it to me tip first. From anyone else's point of view it might have looked like she was threatening me with it.

I sucked in a breath and sniffed. I picked the knife out of her hand with my finger tips; with ease I tossed the knife up into the air and snatched the handle before it could fall. It was a small knife, no smaller than a fruit knife. It weighed like a feather. Unconsciously, I twirled it a few times in my hand and started to peal each potato expertly. I hadn't realized the room grew silent. I winced and looked up. Everyone's eyes were on me. Mags in particular were wide, tiny black dots in pools ofwhite. Bradley's mouthwas open in...Horror? Shock? Amazement?

Sophia looked neutral, though I noticed the slight quiver of her lips. I looked between Tyanna and Cathy, both of them had on ridiculous smiles. I put the cleanly pealed potato and knife down. I pursed my lips and folded my hands in mylap. "What?"

"Holy amaze-balls! Where'd ya learn to do that?" Bradley shouted. I arched a brow, here yes burrowed into mine with... what's a good long word to express this—oh! Astonishment.

"I'm not sure what you mean". I asked innocently. Tyanna nudged my side with her elbow.

"You didn't tell us you were a knives expert! Missy you holding' out on us?" I tried not to grimace and rub my ribs. Still hurts when Elise punched them.

"I'm not a knives expert..."

"Please!". She shouted.

"Language". Mag snapped back at her.

"Then explain what all of that tossing stuff was". She mimicked flicking something in the air with her hands. I shrugged.

"I dunno. I wasn't paying attention so I'm not totally sure what you mean". I started to cube the peeled potatoes.

"What are you doing now?" Bradley asked. I continued to cube and looked up at her.

"Hm?"

"Oh! You are holding out on us!" Tyanna jumped out of her seat, her body shook with energy.

"I'm...cutting up the potatoes?"

"Cu—you're not just cuttin' them". She exclaimed. I reached for the next one and started on that without looking away from her.

"Sure I am," I picked up a large cube chunk and tossed it up and down. "I'm merely cutting the potatoes in cubes so that they all cook and finish at the same time".

"Cubes?" Tyanna and Bradley asked in unison. I opened my mouth to explain, but Cathy beat me to it.

"It's a cooking term. Cube, Julienne, Mince, Shred, etc." She paused to look at me and smiled. "I attended a culinary school during my college years so I know what they all are sweet heart".

Tyanna and Bradley both asked me, "How old are you?" "Seventeen. Why?" Tyanna scoffed and plopped back down on her seat. Bradley shook her head and giggled.

"Cooking master and knives expert...what a strange world we live in". Tyanna said detachedly. Mag chuckled.

"I'm not surprised. It only explains why she has a pair of swords strapped to her back". Tyanna twitched.

"Ooh! I totally didn't notice those till now," She bent back in her seat and traced the black sheath with her finger.

"Are they real?" Bradley asked. I smirked and nodded.

"Tough Japanese steal I can tell ya that. Called, "Tamahagane" which means "Jewel-steal". The forging process takes a long time. By the time I got these bad boys I literally almost peed my pants.Sharp as heck, they could slice throug halmost everything".

It warms my heart to boast about my babies. I sighed dreamily and resumed cutting up the rest of the potatoes. A satisfied smile pasted on my lips.

"How in holy-bells did you get real Katana's?" Tyanna asked incredulously. I pushed aside the finished potato pieces and winked.

"Now that, I'll leave as a mystery".

After a couple of minutes, we've all set ourselves into a steady rhythm. The veggies were stirring in a large steal pot. I placed the platter of sliced apples on the table in the cafe room. A long with the stew is warm bread slathered in butter. I helped Mag carry over the large pot and set it down on a wooden board on the table.

Sophia trailed after her sister like a baby chick, and I thought well ain't that just blasteded sweet Placing both my hands on my hips I huffed.

"Thank the gods! I've finally found you". I looked over my shoulder and found Elise flushed and panting.

"Hey there". I waved.

"Hey' my arse! I've been lookin' all over the god blasted place for you. Do you have any idea how worried me and Nika were? Nearly gave me a freakin heart attack". She grunted and stormed over to me. She was a good two inches taller, plus the added one inch from her boots. She practically towered over me. Don't make me look diminutive E. please don't.

I twisted my lips in order to hide my smile.

"Sorry?"

"Pfft. You better be freakin blasted sorry". She rolled her eyes.

"What were you doing here anyways...?" She traveled off and looked around me. I heard her stomach grumble. I arched a brow and snickered.

"Is that...is that what I think it is?" She whispered.

"Yes E. It's food. They'll be serving in ten minutes". Her green eyes brightened with delight. I shook my head. She's gone.

"Hey". Cathy passed behind us. Her curls bounced with each step.

"Cathy this is Elise. A friend of mine. And—where's Nika?" I asked her.

"Somewhere. Doin' something—everywhere—move". She pushed me aside and stalked into the kitchen.

"She seems nice". Cathy chuckled. I crossed my arms and hummed. "Yeah, word of advice: Don't have any sort of food on you. Specifically during the middle of the day. I won't guarantee you'll survive the attack". She blinked.

"Attack?"

"Oh, E gets a little animalistic when she's hungry. And I'm not always there to keep her on a leash ya know,"I said lightly. "If she starts snarling give her a granola bar or an apple. That'll keep her calm for a bit".

"Are we still talking about a person or do you have a pet dog we don't know about?" Her eyes danced with amusement.

"A person—unfortunately. But, don't tell her I said that. She's a bit sensitive about it yeah?"

There was a loud crash and a piercing shriek coming from the kitchen. Cathy dropped the paper cups on the floor and raced into the kitchen. I followed behind, one hand lightly gripping the sword handle. Once inside, the group of women were clustered towards the back. I stepped cautiously close to them.

"Calm down". Bradley's voice shouted out. I could hardly hear her over the screeching coming from...Tanni.

Blasted that girl could scream, I may lose my hearing after this.

I looked over Mags thick shoulder, Tanni was on the floor. She had her arms wrapped around her knees, slowly rocking back and forth. The screams died down to whimpers.

"What happened?" I asked Mag. She looked over at me and dismissed it with a wave of her hand.

"When she went to place the leftover food in the pantry, we heard a crash and the girl started screaming bloody-murder," She rolled her dark eyes and jerked her thumb towards the shelving unit in the pantry. "We found a hold in the wall. I'd guess she got spooked by a rat or something. She's a blasteded drama queen is all"

I wasn't sure whether to laugh or...laugh. A rat? She got spooked by a rat?

All that screaming over at in yarserodent who's more scared of her than she was of it?

I scanned the group and found Elise hunched over. Her shoulders shook with restrained laughter. Everyone else was trying to either calm Tanni down or look for the rat. I offered to patch the hole up with duck tape and cloth.

172

"That would be a good idea Jade, thank you". Cathy said. She patted Tanni's back and coddled her lightly. As if she were a frightened child. I tried not to snort. Ooh...Tanni can't be one of those wussy types right? God, I hoped not. If this place were to get breached no way in heck was I gonna get stuck with a wussy girl like that. That's wayyy too much responsibility. Uh uh noway ma'am.

After that little scene, everyone cleaned up the kitchen. By then people started to trickle into the cafe room. Definitely more men, a few families, and fewwomen. Unease started to prickle thebase of my neck, I absently rubbed it to make it go away.

I spotted Elise holding on to Nikas arm in a death grip. I don't want to know I met them half way,Nika had on a blank expression; boredom?

While Elise's face flushed with restrained anger. Don't ask Jade "You found her! Congrats". I pat Elise's shoulder, trying to calm her down. Those green orbs burned into mine, and I instinctively took a step back. Ooh, she's mad... "And a good thing too," I sucked in a breath when Elise shoved Nika between the both of us. "I really don't trust the people here jade—well some of them—still, it ain't safe for me, you, or Nika".

Don't you dare ask?

"Why? What happened"? God Blasted!

Nika sighed with exasperation. She crossed her arms and gave me and Elise a look.

"Nothing,she'sjustoverreacting".

"Overreacting?" Elisesnapped.

"Keep it down E". I whispered, I looked around us. Most of the people in the room haven't noticed our little group yet. But some closest to us overheard and quieted their own chatters.

"My god Elise, it was only a bottle. Like...I had one sip. It's not like I chugged the whole blasted thing". Nika breathed. I stilled and looked at her with raised brows.

"Uh huh, I saw that. But that doesn't change the fact that you had liquor. Do you have any idea what that would do to your body? Especially during times like this? What if you got sick or something and you needed medicine for it or...or—ooh!" Elise shook her head vigorously, she shoved her hands in her pockets, biting her lower lip. I gave her a minute to collect herself. These sibling fights aren't rare and at times I find myself enjoying their little squabbles. I'm not a good friend...apparently. Nika threw her hands into the air and scoffed. "Sis! I'm fine okay?

It was a sip. I just wanted to know how it would taste, give me a little room to breathe Blasted. And if you haven't noticed, we live in a fudged up world now. So I'd worry about dying from those undead mongrels outside, than worrying about me taking a baby sip from some low grade alcohol!" I squinted my eyes at that.

And really, I had to agree with Nika. I know Elise was just being a little overprotective. Okay, really overprotective. But can you blame her? Nika is her only little sister and I would be acting the same way if I had a little bro or sis. Moments passed, and finally after pacing in place for agood five minutes, Elise drew out a long breath.

"I'm sorry". She said sheepishly to us both. Then she looked at the people gathered around the room. There were still some on lookers but, everyone else paid more attention to themselves or the food in front of them. I grinned at her. Nika squeezed Elise's hand lightly to comfort her. And now...it's over. For now.

"Alrighty then, now that you guys are good to go, you wanna get some grub?" I asked them. Elise coughed once to hide her obviously hungry tummy, and began walking towards the line for food. Nika skipped beside me, her eyes sparkling with mischief. I cocked my head in thought then glanced over at her.

"What kind of alcohol did you take a "sip" from?" I asked be mused. She eyed me for a minute, the corners of her lips curling into an impish grin.

"Good ol' Jack D's". I nearly tripped on my feet. She dashed into line along with Elise. I scratched the back of my head, a throaty chuckle past my lips.

"Low grade' my arse".

Chapter 22

I f I gotta be honest—even without enough salt—the stew was pretty tasty. It wasn't as loud as one would expect, especially considering half the room was filled towards the corners with people. Most of the families stayed in one corner of the room, mingling to one another.The other was silent. Most kept to themselves. We sat on one of the tables closest to the far right wall of the room. Nika chewed on an apple slice, nibbling lightly. Elise had gone out to fetch half of our supplies—as a thank you for the people's' "hospitality". I turned in my seat, facing out I stretched my legs. I moaned softly at there lease of tension around my knee caps.

"How long have your knees been aching?" Nika asked. I crossed my arms and tucked them behind my head.

"Hm, since three weeks ago—I think," I glanced at my left knee and sighed when I saw that the skin around bone had turned a light shade of red." ‹Swellings not too bad... wait for winter, then start to worry".

I laughed it off. Nika looked between me and my knees, concern etched on her face. I chuckled and pat her head.

"I'll be fine. If it starts to irritate me I'll wrap ‹em up okay?"

"Sure". I gave her head a final pat, then re-crossed my arms across my chest. I have this joke where, I feel like I'm aging too quickly. My mom's told me I was just being overly dramatic, but I think otherwise. My bones would occasionally creak and groan around specific seasons. Especially my knees. Sure, I used to run every morning—still do but for an other reason besides exercise— my knees would protest at acertain point.And very rarely, they'd give out from overuse.

The best thing to do, would be to massage them every other day, stretch before moving, and wrap them with cloth.

Ever since cutting those potatoes a while ago, the need to cut something up has been nudging the back of my mind. I uncrossed and re-crossed my legs, my body longed to move—or something along those lines. Nika was braiding her hair, the gray colored hair tie caught between her teeth.

"Relax". She said. I groaned in response.

"I can't relax—my body refuses to relax. I wanna run or something!" She giggled.

"Then run or something. No one's stopping you".

"But like, if I start sprinting around the building people will think I've gone and lost my marbles". I sighed heavily. Nika straightened in her seat and poked my cheek.

"Too late for that dude. People already think you're weirder than weird. So, run—jump. Do whatever your heart desires". I grabbed her finger and looked at the skin around the nail. It was reddened and calloused from our journey.

"Thanks for the support,Ni-Ni". She snatchedherhandback and glared at me.

"We've talked about this".

"Hm?" I leaned back on my elbows and observed the ceiling above us.

"No one calls me Ni-Ni anymore. That rule doesn't permit you to use it again". I yawned and she snarled back.

"Sure, sure...yeah okay". I waved a hand at her. I felt her anger rise, then suddenly drop. It happened so abruptly, I chanced a peek at her. The orange flecks scattered about the jade backdrop of her eyes glittered. Her eyes were staring ahead.

"Nika?" I flicked her bangs. No response.

"You, gecko? Are you Earth bound, yes or nah?" I

asked. "Hem". She squeaked. I raised a brow. What

now? "Dude...you alright there?"

She spun around to face me. Taking my head between her hands, she jerked my attention to the front near the main doors.

"How the heck did you miss that?" She shriek—whispered in my ear. My jaw dropped, I wasn't even sure I wanted to pick it up off the floor after this.

Standing under the archway of the doorway stood such a fine assembly of good looking—nay, spicy looking young specimens my seventeen years has ever witnessed. Said jaw that currently laid on the floor, lifted up and reattached itself to my face. That was when I noticed a couple of girlish murmurs in the background.

Holy heck bottoms! Again, why now of all times?!

And of course leading said spicy mass was Evan. He'd changed his white t-shirt to a simple gray Henley. The first two buttons left open, exposing his tanned collar bones. His hair looked charmingly messy. As If he'd been running his hands through it all day. I'd like to run my hands all over that body insetI shook my head, denying my obscene thoughts. Stop thinking about stuff like that Blasted!

"God, fates such a biatch". I flinched at the sound of Elise's voice beside me. How she snuck over beside me without my knowing, I'll never comprehend.

"Indeed". Nika agreed dreamily. I noticed a familiar head of spiky dirty blond hair in the group.

"Ain't that Danny, Samantha's brother?" I asked. Elise squinted her eyes and nodded.

"Yup, that's him".

"He's cute". I said.

"Yup". Both Nika and Elise said in unison. There were other guys, all close to one another's age. Yet, all I saw was Evan and his god blasted Henley. Curse you Henley's.

What I wouldn't give to trace the bone lining his jaw and all the way down— I bit my lip in order to stop my wandering thoughts. I groaned louder this time—infrustration. Elise sat on top of the table beside me and snickered.

"It's starting".

"Don't E. Just don't". I said. She placed her hand on my shoulder and squeezed.

"I can hear it in your voice Jade. Like I said, the more you deny it, the worse it'll get". I bit back are tort that would have made my trigger happy uncle proud. That's when "He" spotted me amidst the crowd. I sucked in a breath. The words lodged in my stupid throat. That freakin grin of his was gleaming so blasted brightly I wanted to smile back just—just to do that. If I had a penny for every time this guy's made me speechless—much less uncommunicative I would have had at least a hundred by now.

He started to walk towards us. Enemy target approaching!

Orders captain?

The imaginary force inside my head shouted at me.

Four feet till impact! Battle stations!

His long strides only made those four feet, a few inches

shorter. Ready men, brace yourselves!

Once he stopped in front of us—like at least a foot away. I kept my head straight. Leaning it slightly to the side I focused on a dirt covered spot against the wall. I tried to appear casual, lazed like.

"How'd you like the food? Cathy and the girls are great cooks huh?" His voice was low,and ever so slightly I could feel the rumble emit from his chest, making my body shiver involuntarily. I tensed my jaw, waiting for my mouth to function properly.

"Mhm! It was sooo delicious". Nika got in between and answered for me. Thanks Nika.

"I heard you helped out in there. Tyanna wouldn't stop blabbering on about how you handled the knife like a...what was it she called you—ah, a "Knives Expert?"

I finally grew some balls and looked up at him. He stood there.

All six feet and some. Oh my, my how those stormy eyes ragged on once he met my gaze. Its hurricane season all three hundred and sixty days a year in those eyes!

I heard Elise cough. Her hand still squeezing my shoulder reassuringly.

"Oh, yeah well I might've "skillfully" cut some potatoes but, I wouldn't go so far as to call myself an expert".

He tilted his head to the side. The grin grew wider.

"Am I to assume then, that the rumors of your expertise in knives are false?" He asked. The tone of his voice lowered even more.I felt a bit ballsy and annoyed and—other things that should never be mentioned!

So I said, "I wouldn't say I'm a master with knives, but others things...I won't contest to". I felt Nika turn in her seat, her head sunk a top the table. Elise released her hold on my shoulder and covered her mouth with her hand. Her body trembled.

I looked back to Evan, the grin was gone from his face. A subtle curve of his lips, head cocked to the side. The raging storm in his eyes only darkened. Heavy gray clouds promised sever rain. OhI know that look! Don't look at me like that blasted you!

I then rethought my choice of words. My insides screamed at my stupidity.

Why does everything I say sound profane? Is that like a habit or something?!

Evan took a step closer to me and my neck ached from looking up. So instead I stood up from my seat. Straightening to my full height, my five foot six to his six and over.

"Interesting". Was all he said in response. I felt the tips of his boots poke mine. We were so close—too close. I could feel his hot breath across my face. He narrowed his eyes at me.

"Then the rumors are...partially true". I inhaled, my nose tingled from his scent. Pine, sun, all man through and through. Ah heck, I can't help myself.

Yes, my girly hormones are on high alert, and yes I'm trying my blastededest to control my inner demon, (freaking lusty demon) and just inhale all that is Evan. God! I wish Elise would pull me back and bind my arms before I pull that blasted head of this down and attack his lips.

"How's your pinky bytheway?" I stopped breathing for a second.

Then inhaled and exhaled.

"It's fine". I answered.

"That's good". Yes, yes that's good and all but if you're done please distance yourself from me. I maybe holding the reigns but, they're slipping every second. Meanwhile, I traced the slight curve of his arched brows—admiring the view up close and personal again—and I caught him observing my lips. Mylips.

Oh bud, I wouldn't do that if I were you... I stepped back and caught myself at the table's edge. I cleared my throat,

"Elise, Nika we need to regroup and have a meeting". I cringed inwardly at the huskiness of my voice.

I felt them glance at me, then nod. I nodded back causally and stepped to the side. Grabbing my back holster and katanas, I hitched them over my shoulder. That blasted grin was back on full power, as Evan moved to the opposite side, my stupid arm decides to graze his in return. The skin around my arm tingled, I clenched my jaw.

"I could see I'm clearly being dismissed". He chuckled.

"That, you are sir". I began walking towards the open doors. I heard Nika and Elise fall in behind me a moment later.

Chapter 23

Irounded the trucks' drivers' side then to the back. Elise opened the   back door and hopped on. Both Nika and Elise sat side by side on the ledge. I stood in the center of the space, facing them.

Earlier in the day Jason and a few others allowed us to use this space as ours—for the duration of our stay I mean. Same room as the rest of the building, large windows covered in dirt. High ceilings, loose fixtures swung lazily. A 5 minute walk from the main hall. The day grew darker and we lit a few battery powered lanterns about the room.

I paced around the room, arms crossed tightly against my chest.

"How long are we gonna hole up in here?" I asked them.

"Not sure, maybe a few days". Elise said lightly, humming under her breath.

"A few days...2's enough to kill me already". Draining really. I muttered. Nika swung her legs back and forth.

"I like it here". She said.

"Me too.'Foods good". Elise added.

"You're content anywhere as long as there's food". I said back. She huffed.

"Not true".

"Oh so true E."

"Whatever". She pouted. I bit my lip and paced in a circle. All this restless energy will start to annoy me the longer I don't do something.

"What about making allies—enemies? Yousaid so yourself E. We don't have time for unnecessary company". She leaned back, wide eyes on me.

"I did say that didn't I?" She paused and I waited for her to continue, but after a moment her lips stayed sealed.

"And...?"

"I've decided to change that rule". I gawked at her.

"What?"

"Times are tough. And now that we've stumbled upon these people, I thought...well why not? I mean from what I could see, they're being nice so far".

"Yeah...I thought so too. But, what if one day all their kindness just turned out to be a front? And we'll have to fight the very people we trusted in the beginning". She stared at me then pursed her lips in thought. She shrugged,

"We'll cross that bridge if and when we get to it". My jaw tensed, I turned my back on them. If I stay here any longer...I might convulse from the inside out.

"There's another reason for your irritation". Nika said this as a statement—or maybe a question?

"Not really, I just..." I shoved a hand through my hair and sighed.

"It's about Evan ain't it?" Elise asked lightly. Her voice was so quiet if it weren't for the general silence in the room I wouldn't have heard her ask that.

I spun around to face her and glared.

"Elise..."

"Oh it is!" Nika shrieked excitedly. She hopped off the truck and waved her hands in the air. "Please don't". Elise rushed at me. I didn't have enough time to block her assault. She clutched my head between her hands then shook it furiously.

"Mh...Ehm! Gu?" I grit my teeth, trying my blastededest to get out of her hold. Her grip only tightened the more I struggled.

"Now you listen to me young lady! I'm not gonna deal with your 'it's complicated' or 'I don't have time for this' bullshiznit! The longer you wait this out, the worse you're frustration will get". She stopped shaking my head and stared into my eyes. Her cheeks were slightly flushed and her eyes sparkled. Oh... you're having fun with this aren't you?

"God you're redundant! Would you stop going back to that?" I whined.

"Because silly," She tsked. "I see the way you both look at each other. Sure it's only been –what? A day and a half since you two have met?" I nodded slowly.

"Yes so, I can tell that he's as much into you as you are to him. It's both gross and cute to see you two bicker. And to be honest..." she flicked my nose with a free hand. "It gets a little too hot and heavy, know what I'm saying'?"

My jaw drew slack and I slumped in defeat. Besides the hot and heavy remark she's the mature and smart one here, and I hate that she's right. Most of the time... But I won't admit shiznit that easily.

"Jade, please...please think about this. When are you ever gonna get a chance like this? As much as it pains me to let you go, I kinda trust him... for some reason. You know?"

She loosened her hold and dropped her hands to her sides. I chewed on my lower lip, looking anywhere but at the one person who's always tried to protect me—keep me away from guys. Now I have this...this other person begging me to take a chance. I may be being a little dramatic. And yeah, this ain't about to turn into an innocently sweet romance. But why the heck not. God help me.

"Okay". I muttered.

"What was that?"

"Okay! Fine, I-I'll try to um...I don't know-" I scratched the back of my neck nervously.

"You'll do what you always do jade. Believe me when I say,He won't be able to resist ya". Oh! And she has the audacity to wink right after she said all that.

"Yeah okay. A-are you done now?" I took a step back.

"Mhm". She plopped back down on her seat. Nika twirled around the room. The motion making me a bit nauseous.

"What time is it?" I asked, hoping to divert the current topic of our conversation.

"Uh, 7...no, 8:25 pm". Elise was leaning over the back seat to view the dashboards' clock.

"Blasted, it's early".

"I don't know about you guys but, I'm gonna hit the hay' nights". Nika strolled over to one corner of the room—near the windows and dropped a rolled up queen sized comforter on the ground. The bright multi-checkered fabric stood out in contrast to the gray tones around us. She added a small pillow to her pile and like she said, "Hit the hay".

"I call first watch". I said before Elise could counter.

"Jade, when's the last time you slept?"

"Before we got here". I smoothed the creases on my white tank top.

"How long though?" I thought for a moment.

"20 minutes". She opened her mouth to speak, then closed it.

"20...minutes".

"Right-O". I tightened the belts on my back holster and walked away. The half crescent moon rose high in the sky.I could only make out the lining of its curved shape from within the grit covered windows. I took my time walking around the building. The room we occupied had a set of twin metal doors that locked from the inside.

We had no key for the lock but, I was able to find a crowbar to nudge in between the handles. The lights were off in the hallway. I wasn't sure how much time passed before my body grew weary.

"Wake up, wake up". I muttered to myself. My body refused to walk any longer, with a sigh I walked to the side, the wall next to the twin doors leading to our room and slid down to the floor. Resting my head on the hard concrete wall, I readjusted the back holster to a more comfortable position. I bent one of my knees to my chest and wrapped an arm around it. The other lay flat on the dirty floor.

I could sleep. Yeah I could, but I needed to keep an eye out. I know that Nika and Elise trust these people. But it's only been a day, we can't know for sure if they are who they say they are. I'm not a people person, and my certainty on the whole situations a bit out of sorts. The most I could do for them, is to protect them at all costs. They may be the only people left in my life right now... my mother. I know it's not best to think negatively, but what if she didn't make it to an evacuation squad? What if those bloody nail marks I saw on the doorway...were hers and she...?

"No". I thumped my head against the wall behind me. I shouldn't think like this, she's fine. For all I know, she might be sleeping in a soft cot somewhere safe, away from all this madness.

Away from all this stupid shiznit. I clenched and unclenched my hands.

"She wouldn't die that easily". I mumbled under my breath. I took out my necklace, I had tucked it underneath my tank to keep it from getting snatched from all the action. It squeezed the small gold cross, the tiny intricate butterfly design—engraved on the other side—was soft against my fingertips. I had it made for my mother's birthday a year ago. She had been so happy to get it. I remember the wide smile she gave me when she unwrapped the red ribboned box on that day. I knew what to get her. She always loved butterflies so it was a pretty easy gift to buy.

The last day I went to school, I decided to wear it—just to wear it. I'm glad that I did.

I felt the dampness around my eyes, and shut them before the blasted tears could fall. I would not cry, not now, not ever. So I clutched the golden memory in my hands and fell into a dreamless sleep.

The next morning, the three of us wasted time by going over ourplans. Since discovering this new safe compound, we'd had to move a few things around, sort through new roads. Elise picked up a map of the state and another for the country. We've pin pointed some cleared off roads, marked each in black sharpie.

The only sounds in the space around us emitted from the Hummers radio. We would get white noise most of the time. On specific hours of the day, reports would fill us in on what's going on out there. The city was still a no-go. Reports concluded that to any survivors roaming the state to stay clear of the cities and big communities.

I've opted out looking for anything in the city, but Nika was really hype on about how there might beguns there or abandoned pawn shops.

We sat in a circle around the map of the state. The corners pinned down by small rocks found around the room. I sat cross legged and leaned back on the palms of my hands.

"What about that corner street downtown? Tree St." Elise asked, she took out a red sharpie and began to draw in the street with ink. I eyed the map questioningly.

"The dude on the reports said, that it was closed off".

"Oh". She popped the cap off the black sharpie and drew an 'X' on the red inked street. From what the reports could inform us on, most of the coastal areas in the country took the worst of the infection. New York, Washington, California and other large cities and towns were blocked off. Evacs were having a hard time trying to round up survivors. The rest of the world was suffering just as much as we were. I worry for my Aunt and Uncle in Atlanta.They both work for computer systems in the CDC, so I suppose they're safe there.

Elise circled the outer perimeter of Chicago, and calculated our current location; distance from the city to where we were.

"I'll never understand that longitude, latitude crap". I bent my head from side to side. Elise glanced at me and smirked.

"Aren't ya glad I actually know how to do this kind of stuff?" She saidhaughtily.Ichucked a crumpled up granola barwrapper at her, the plastic bounced off the tip of her nose. Nika snorted and fell over laughing. Elise glared at me but the corners of her mouth started to curve upwards slightly.

"Figuring coordinates is easy Jade". She said continuing to mark the other streets. One ear on the radio the other on us.

"I hate math," She gave me an odd look. I shrugged. "Looking at numbers for too long makes my head hurt". She sighed,

"It doesn't take that much to figure It out". "I'm impatient". She stared it me for moment, then shook her head.

"Aren't we all"?

"Mhm".

She traced street after street in red sharpie, bordering our current position.

"I'll mark this as a safe zone, and mark along each place we clear out on the road".

I unfolded my legs and stretched them out, the bones groaned, the muscles rigid.

"Let's leave a sign—or a mark on it. Signaling to anyone who passes by that it's a secured safe zone". I looked towards Nika and nodded in agreement.

"That's sounds like a good idea". I looked up at the ceiling in thought.

"We're gonna need bright paint and a giant arse brush". Elise giggled.

"Or better yet, let's see if we can score some spray paint". Nika added excitedly.

"We'll get to try out our hands on graffiti for the first time". I said absently.

"Ooh, and we won't get in trouble, awesome!" Nika fist pumped the air. Elise sat back and viewed the map. After a while she sighed in contentment and recapped the two sharpies.

"That'll do for now I guess. Until we can get more information". She said. I looked at the red and black marks on the map. Some streets were filled with black—telling us that, that area was off limits or blocked. The red, marked pass able roads. One area of the map was enclosed in red and black sharpie, outlining a square. For the letters, 'SZ' scrawled above it.

"Looks good". I said.

"Yep". She said back.

I lied back on the floor, my arms crossed behind my head.

"What time is it?" I asked. I heard scuffling, and a door creaking open.

"Five past 7 in the morning".

"Ugh". I groaned.

"When did they say breakfast begins?" Elise asked.

Did I detect worry?

"7..." I said quietly. I heard a gasp then the doors behind us slammed open and closed. All I felt was a slight shifting of air.

"Was that Elise?" I asked Nika.

"Yup".

"She's a trooper". I said.

"Yup". A pause.

"Youwanna get breakfasttoo? Andalso make sure she doesn't clear them out". She snickered in response. With a grunt, I propped my self in a sitting position then used my stiffleg muscles to stand up. Nika was already walking out of the room. I glided past her and walked briskly down the hallway.

"Wait up". She skipped up beside me. By the time we got to the cafe, the place was packed just like last night.It looked like everyone wasin the samespots as the day before. I spotted Elise already sitting at the table we took to last time. She shoveled something that resembled oatmeal into her mouth. Not giving a shiznit about how ridiculous she looks to the others, I salute you.

"Esh, that girl could put it away". A low whistle sounded behind me. I looked over my shoulder and found a familiar pair of dark brown eyes. Mag gave me a quick smile and gestured towards Elise.

193

"Yeah, that's how she is". She chuckled.

"Every time she eats?"

"In general". I said back.

"Fascinating". She replied back with a cackle. I grinned right back at that. Fascinating was the correct term for how Elise was uh, devouring? I'm not totally sure.

I watched as Nika hopped up to the end of the line. We had changed our clothes to clean ones to appear...I don't know, more approachable?

I guess walking around covered in dark crusted bloody clothing and a pair of very sharp swords attached to one's back would scare the pants off of anyone.

She was wearing a large gray graphic t-shirt, the words 'Freak on the loose' printed in black letters on the front, and a pair of cut off jean shorts which personally I think are abit too short. But I'm not her mother so, I have no reason to critique her outfit choices.

The back of the shirt was tied with a rubber band and tucked into the back.

Elise was wearing a form fitting green V-neck short sleeved shirt. And a pair of dark jean shorts. Her black clad combat boots were crossed underneath the table. Her hair was tied up high on herhead,ano-nonsense kind of ponytail. Although some strands had escaped from—what I could guess— when she raced for the cafe earlier. I shook my head.

As for me, all I did was change my white tank to a brand spanking new one and changed my jean shorts for a clean pair, the ends were 'distressed' stylishly. Looking hot even during an apocalypse.

Okay, I kinda have to admit my clothes hugged my body in certain areas that are totally not family-friendly. And again, I don't have anyone to impress. Although there is a certain someone I kinda want to impress.

I muttered. Mag looked at me curiously. I sighed and walked forward. Once I got to the food table I grabbed a small paper bowl and filled it with raisins and sliced green apple pieces. I walked back to the table and plopped down on the cool seat.

"That all ya gonna eat?" Elise asked, the question muffled by the half chewed food in her mouth. I leaned forward on my forearms giving her a pointed look.

"What?"

"Just because the world's going to shiznit—

" "Halfway through dude".

"-Doesn't mean you get a free pass for poor table manners". She blinked and giggled.

"You're funny". She continued to shovel the contents of her meal into her mouth. I grimaced with slight disgust.

"I don't remember that term being anywhere close to my described character". She wiped her mouth the back of her hand and pushed the empty bowl to the side.

"I beg to differ". She replied back coolly.

"Yeah well, you're opinion in the matter rather— you're "assumption" of me sucks". I snarled back. She slapped the table top and howled with laughter.

"Says the girl who finds slicing the limbs off of people enjoyable".

"Bodies...those things are no longer considered people". I said back.

"Hm, you've got a point".

"And I don't find it enjoyable". I picked up an apple slice and chewed on it slowly. The sour juiciness stung my taste buds. She rolled her eyes.

"Bullshiznit. You love it and ya know it". I eyed the space over her shoulder, not wanting to meet her eyes.

"Yeah okay..." I chucked a raisin at her, she put her hand up and the shriveled piece bounced off it. She grinned back at me.

"You wanna spar today? It's been a while". She fiddled with the tips of her pony tail.

We haven't been training for some time, not like we haven't neglected our muscles—oh the shiznit out there's doing more than our usual 2 hour sparring sessions.

"You've space big enough for us?" I asked "Our room duh. We can just move the truck closer to the back gate and we'll have enough room to kick each other's arses with".

I snickered at that.

"Well? What are we still sitting here for"? I was so ready to strip off this blasted tank top. It was just too blasted hot in our room. Add to the fact we had no source of air condi- tioning, or fans. And the meager breeze drifting in through the few broken windows did nothing to cover the sweltering heat.

I was sweating so much, the tank became translucent and clung to my body like a second skin. I had propped my twins by the wall—close by of course just in case. We've been at it for only an hour and my legs and arms groaned in pain. I waved to Elise, signaling a 5 minute break. She was also drenched in sweat, bright red splotches covered her cheeks. She grunted in agreement and bent over breathing in and out heavily.

"You got in a few good hits. Not bad". I said re-tying my damp hair with a small rubber band. She looked up and huffed.

"Yeah, but it was even harder to dodge you're hit's. I swear," She shook her head and held out her arms, closer inspection showed harsh red marks the size of my fists decorated her entire arm starting from the forearm to her shoulder. I was sure she had marks all over besides her arms.

"Sorry".

"'Sorry' yeah well, I'm gonna have purple spots all over me in a couple 'an hours might as well wrap 'em upnow".

"We'll have towork on your form more, dodging drills again.I hate seeing you beat up like that". She glared at me.

"Ooh! Ain't you just a doll-" she said in her famous 'I'm pissed so I'll go southern on you drawl'

"And oh! You even took the courtesy not to maw ma face in in the process. You should na'ave". I just stared at her waiting for her to calm down. I gave her my best smile and tossed a piece of cut off cloth at her. She snatched it from the air and wiped the sweat from her reddened face.

"I do what I do the best I can". Smirking I walked around her in a circle. Her eyes never leaving me.

"You ready?" I cracked my neck and kept my hands relaxed at my sides. She didn't respond instead she threw the moist cloth at me—as a distraction I guess—and lunged at me. I stepped slightly to the right, she spun around and swung her right arm aiming for my face. I blocked her hit with my elbow and jumped back when she lifted her leg and kicked the empty space I was once in.

We danced around each other. Our fists connected every once in a while. I was so in the zone I barely heard the doors slam open. Elise ducked low and went for my abdomen, her left hand jabbed hard and fast. I doubled over but recovered quickly. She tried to swipe my legs from under me, but at the last second I jumped up twisting in mid air, my bare foot collided with her shoulder. In the beginning we opted for bare feet so as to "lessen" the damage. I heard awince from behind me. I looked over my shoulder. Nika was hovering by the open doorway. Light sparkled in her eyes. Behind her stood a group of people, I immediately recognized a pair of startling gray eyes. Oh no... I grabbed Elise's hand as it flew for my face. She jerked violently and tried to use her free hand to release my vise on her wrist.

"C'mon! No fair. You know you have an advantage because you're more muscled—ease up!" She whined. I could tell she was exhausted and I'd bet her shoulder took the brunt ofmy attack.

I stared her down—she was bent at little at the waist, she was taller than me normally but she was tired and amusingly bratty—I whispered,

"Cool it we have an audience". She blew out a breath and glanced over my shoulder. I would have been laughing my arse off for how big Elise's eyes had bulged out if it weren't for our unexpected guests currently watching us from the doorway.

"D-do I look as bad as I feel?" She asked weakly. I released her wrist as she tried to tame the escaped tendrils of blond hair back into the pony tail. I turned around slowly towards them.

"We both look like shiznit I'm sure. So stop messing with your hair". I whispered back. I exhaled gently and went to wipe the sweat on my upper lip. At this point I didn't really care that these people were getting a peep show of my stomach. It ain't like those feminine tummies you'd normally see. The hem of my tank rose the higher I went. I've got a well-toned 4-pack; from extensive workouts and training. The few scars I have lightened up and crisscross behind my back. I looked up and flinched in wardly when I saw Evan roaming up all over that naked space. His eyes narrowed and stared at a certain spot below my ribcage. Like the biohazard tat?

I had gotten that a year ago. Just for the heck of it. To this day my mom has never found out about it. Once he settled on my face I could have sworn that trademark grin grewwider.

I heard Elise clear her throat, I let go of the hem and smoothed it down over my stomach. I actually have two. The black biohazard under my rib cage; the size of a Ping-Pong ball. And the more recent addition right behind my neck. It wasn't anything fancy just three connecting infinity symbols made in the shape of a small triangle. I chose those wisely because once the inks in your skin, it's there for life—unless you have enough money to remove it surgically—yeah, it's there forever.

I shook my arms out, they lay lax by my sides. God what is with this silence?

"You guys were sparing without me?" Nika's high pitched voice broke the quiet. I looked to Elise who shrugged.

"We didn't know if you wanted to. I mean, you were still eating..."

"You could have, you know? Waited!" She shook her armsin the air. I blinked and walked over to the Hummer.

"Are both of y'all that impatient?'

"Yes Nika we are. We didn't want to wait for your slow arse to finish eatin-" "That's still not fair you didn't wait".

"Life's not fair in general. Get over it".

I grabbed ahalf filledwater bottle and chugged theclear liquid down. It was lukewarm from the heat, but I didn't care. Water is water right? Tossing the empty bottle aside I walked back to the two arguing sisters.

They went silent once I got in between them.

"If you still wanna go, I'm cool with sparing with you". I told Nika.

"What...really?" Her speckled eyes dazzled with excitement. I nodded with a smirk.

"You might even need some practice anyways," I walked over to the open space and took my stance lifting my chin.

"C'mon then". She looked to Elise who shook her head then nodded once. Nika squealed, then tore her boots off. Along with her— aw, rainbow colored socks—and sprinted forward. I was ready by the time her fist connected with my forearm. I clenched my teeth at the sharp pain radiating from the impact spot. She hopped back and swung down aiming to take my legs from under me. Nika was tricky to read. Unlike her sister, whose movements are controlled and coordinated, Nika was just...

random. Her punches ranged from right hooks to quick-slow jabs. High kicks to sweeps. She was flexible so she can dodge fairly easily. She went in for a high kick. I grabbed her ankle at the last second and tugged. She flung to the side, she groaned from the heavy landing then immediately sat up in a crouch.

"Easy..." I heard a voice behind me murmur. I ignored that when she pounced forward. I blocked her assault as best I could.

In the end we had to stop when my knee finally gave, forcing me to kneel on the ground. I focused on my breathing.

Deep breath in, hold 1...2...3...exhale slowly. I continued to do this exercise until my pounding heart settled. I felt a hand on my shoulder; much too large to be Elise's or Nika's.

I peeked up and found and those...freaking eyes. The gap in his Henley gave me a tantalizing view of sun exposed skin. I'm seriously considering binding my hands together whenever I'm around him.

"You alright?"

"Yeah, yeah just...just give me a moment". I fought to keep my control on lock down. The high adrenaline rushing through my system didn't help in any way. I rubbed my now red throbbing knee and got up—as gracefully as I could manage—using my back muscles for support. I stretched my arms high above my head and bit back a yawn. It was too early to rest but blasted am I tired.

Evan was still looking at me, his brow furrowed slightly with concern.

"Amazing".

"Hm?" I glanced towards Evan, who had both his hands shoved into his front pockets. The pose was disarmingly boyish. Add with his ever curling hair falling against his forehead. He chuckled and nodded at the open space.

"You're well trained, so I said 'Amazing'".

"Yeah, I guess". I shrugged. He cocked his head to the sidewith a question in his eyes. I withdrew a rubber band from my hair and shook it out. The curling dark hair tangled. I brushed through it with my fingers. Then shoved the annoying bangsback, they only flopped back on over my eyes. I picked at the damp tips absently. It was getting longer; I usually had my hair shoulder length or bob cut. But they now grew past my shoulders, ending in a disarray.

I should ask Elise to whip up some scissors.

"You guess? Those were combatant moves," he took out his hands and with a move so smooth I barely blocked it, he gently clipped my jaw. My right hand was up before you could have— from the position—broken or dislocated the jaw bone. My face was calm on the outside but on the inside

I was shrieking like a howler monkey. Holy smokes! That was hecka close "Good," He murmured under his breath. Then he backed up— more like inched back and chuckled. I raised a brow and crossed my arms. The look he was giving me made my muscles twitch.

"Where'd you learn?" He asked. He leaned back casually.

"Facilities, programs, after that was self-taught," I waved a hand at Elise and Nika "I taught them a thing or two...you never know when you'll need 'em". I tried not to salivate when he bit the corner of those blasted tasty lookin' lips.

"I see". He nodded.

"You're form was pretty good too". I said back.

"Jason taught some of us a little bit of everything. He was in the military you know".

I nodded in agreement.

"Mhm. You could tell by his stance. The air around him is intense and controlled," I shook my head in admiration, "aura leakin'out". You'd be blind as heck if you couldn't tell". I snickered. "I'm with you on that". He said back. We stood there in silence for a moment. Were it not for the shuffling of feet on dirt covered ground I could have been ogling Evan for hours.

I would if I could.

I sighed heavily and turned towards the noise. Both Elise and Nika were mingling with the group under the doorway—which I honestly forgot about.

"That you're crew?" I asked Evan playfully. Amusement glittered in his eyes, he chuckled.

"I suppose you could call 'em that". I tilted my head to the other side and pursed my lips. I looked past his broad shoulder and instantly rolled my eyes at the sight.Heck yeah Evan was one fine piece of Man, but I still could not believe the insanely, unnecessary collection of dudes before me. All hail theapocalypse!

Elise was standing slightly to the side, nodding her head whenever she feels compelled to. A light blush spread above her cheeks. Whereas Nika talked animatedly to the group.Onepersoninparticular. I again recognized that head of spiky dirty blond hair. "Jade! come over here". Elise hollered. I giggled and peeked over at Evan—who by the way was still staring at me. A bit creepy but I like the attention he's giving me "Well, I guess we should head on over to them huh".I laughed nervously. He gave me one of those odd looks of his and laughed. He stepped to the side and held out his hand, gesturing towards the group.I walked past him and heard a slight cough behind me. Thank you Elise for oh so announcing the size of my rump for all to hear. You just gave him something to gawk at. And I'm not even sure if I should be ashamed or flattered.

I'm weird.

The end